Lock Down Publications and Ca$h
Presents

A
Thuggish
Passion 2

Love & War

Written By
Ira B

Lock Down Publications
P.O. Box 944
Stockbridge, GA 30281
www.lockdownpublications.com

Like our page on Facebook: Lock Down Publications
www.facebook.com/lockdownpublications.ldp

Stay Connected with Us!

Text **LOCKDOWN** to 22828 to stay up-to-date with new releases, sneak peaks, contests and more...

Like our page on Facebook:
Lock Down Publications

Join Lock Down Publications/The New Era Reading Group

Visit our website:
www.lockdownpublications.com

Follow us on Instagram:
Lock Down Publications

Email Us: We want to hear from you!

Dedication

I dedicated this book to Katherine "Kat" Thomas for always being who you are. You taught me patience and how to "forgive" when I thought I never had it in me. I love you with all my heart. Thank you.

Acknowledgements

I know this might sound crazy to many but I just want to say thank you to my penmanship. Yes. My pen. I live with my pen, it never sleeps. We are a team. I am the brain and it is the voice to the world. My pen is golden. It's part of who I am.

Chapter 1

"What do we have here?" Muttered Romell Butler the instant they turned onto the street. Up ahead he observed the big group of people standing outside Trenika's grandmother's house. But it was what he saw happening at the doorstep of that same house that made him want to crush something.

"Is that nigga on his knees?" Bam said from behind the wheel of the car they were riding in.

"Yep." Romel sneered. Sure enough, there was someone on his bending knee as he held his arms outstretched toward the woman before him. And to his surprise, that woman appeared to be none other than Trenika herself. At the sight of her, Romell began to boil with a deep, dark rage that shook him to the core.

As the car proceeded to ride past the scene Romell never took his eyes off Trenika. Here it was, he hadn't expected to see her after Trenika abandoned her home down in Florida. He expected her to be anywhere where she couldn't be found. Not here at her childhood home experiencing a marriage proposal by some mark who had no clue what he was capable of.

And then she gazed up toward the passing car, locked eyes with him from a distance, gasped, and bolted from the door without a backward glance. Whoever this nigga was proposing to his woman, Romell witnessed the dejected slump of his shoulders as the door closed shut in his face. Romell wanted to laugh at him but was distracted by another face in the group of people standing out front. When he saw Lance, a whole other beast awakened in him. Then he was reminded of their last confrontation and what Lance had done to his family as a result of their beef.

"Somebody's gonna die today," Romell sang as he reached underneath the passenger seat for his MAC-.90 assault weapon. "I need you to circle around, Bam. I'm about to put it down on all their asses," he added grimly.

"Now you're talking my language." Bam nodded and drove up to the next stop sign and circled back around.

Wounding his side window down, Romell eased his body out of the window and sat down upon the inner surface of the door. He pulled his fitted cap low over his eyes and brought up his big gun. Setting the MAC.90 down upon the roof of the car, Romell readied himself for what he knew would no doubt make the evening news.

The moment the car reached its point of attack and Lance looked up at its presence, Romell snarled in his direction and aimed his weapon. Suddenly automatic rounds rang out as Romell mercilessly gunned down everybody in his line of vision of hitting his target.

Twenty-eight rounds later, Romell ducked back into the car and Bam floored it. "Fuck!" Romell punched the glove compartment in frustration, angry that he didn't hit Lance like he wanted to.

The nigga was fast and smart. He separated himself from the others while running in zig zag patterns. Lance didn't even get the opportunity to get off a shot from the gun he drew in his hasty retreat. But Benji did, who Romell had to focus his attention on next. However, he was well aware of the young nigga's participation in the deaths of his loved ones. He was trying to tear Benji's whole head off.

"What happened?" Bam demanded as he put distance between them and the bloody scene behind them.

"Don't worry, brah," said Romell as he sat back against the passenger seat and fired up his Black & Mild cigar. "It's what's about to happen that's really gonna blow your muthfuckin' mind, my nigga."

"Okay. What's about to happen then?" Bam brought the car before a stoplight and looked over at him.

And that's where Romell blew his mind with a bullet straight through his brain. "My bad, brah, but I play for keeps," he said.

***

Trenika was so scared that she snatched Aryanna up and hit the backdoor without stopping to offer her grandmother an explanation for her actions. All she cared about was to get herself and her daughter somewhere safely away from the monster that's haunted her dreams. Seeing Romell just now was a cold reminder of how much her life was still in danger.

When she opened the front door and found Kaedon on one knee, Trenika couldn't believe her eyes. At first she was stunned to the point of speechlessness, then Kaedon said all the words that any woman would have said yes to. But after she laid eyes on Romell, she spoke the words out of fear instead of love. It all happened so fast that Trenika left behind her cellphone and shoes in her escape. She didn't have time to second guess what she should do. Then, when she heard the gunshots exploding behind her, she knew it was Romell and his murderous intent to destroy everything she loved.

Trenika didn't want to die. She heard the petrified screams in the air of her loved ones experiencing Romell's outrage. Her heart squeezed with fear of what tragedy she left behind in the wake of her monster's dark mood.

Behind Grandma Cora's house was a back path that led to a nearby alleyway. Trenika, with Aryanna pressed tightly in her arms, ran up that alley as hard as she could. She made it to the next street over and jetted between two houses that also led to a second alley. People in passing looked up at her like she'd lost her damn mind. Trenika ran and ran until she made it all the way to the other side of the neighborhood. Before long she was barging through the entrance door of a nearby gas station. She asked where she could use the restroom. A minute later Trenika locked herself and her daughter inside the restroom where she slumped down on the floor next to the toilet trying to catch her breath. She was tired from running and scared to death.

"Your feet are bleeding, mommy," Aryanna said with a frown and looked around the restroom for something her mother could use to clean up the blood.

It was then that Trenika realized that she hadn't stopped to put her shoes on. She looked down at her bloody feet and shook her head in dismay. The throbbing sensation kicked in now that her mind was aware of her injuries.

"Here, mommy." Aryanna had managed to pull loose multiple sheets of paper napkins from the dispensary attached to the wall across the room. "You need to clean it so we can get it fixed with some medicine."

"Thank you, baby girl." Trenika accepted the paper napkins.

"Why are we here, mommy? What's going on?" Aryanna had tears in her eyes when she noticed her mother was crying. She reached over and wiped her mother's tears away and told her that everything was going to be alright.

To tell her daughter the truth about Romell would destroy her and the image she had of Kaedon. The only father she knew or would understand was Kaedon and no other man. She couldn't tell Aryanna the truth, but she did say a bad man wanted to hurt them and take her away.

"Daddy won't let that happen, mommy." Aryanna put her hands on her hips in that stubborn way she learned from Trenika. "He won't let nobody hurt us. Call daddy and he'll come get us and protect us."

At the mention of Kaedon and thinking about the look she saw in his eyes when she denied him was heart aching. Trenika would never forget the sorrow she saw in Kaedon's eyes. She had hurt another man that she loved and the pain it was causing her in the process ran deep.

"Daddy will do what he can," Trenika replied. She wondered if her daughter caught the shakiness in her voice. Wherever Kaedon was, there was no telling what was going through his mind. She wanted to call him so bad but something in her heart warned her not to. Trenika only wanted to get as far away from those she cared for because Romell won't hesitate killing them to get to her.

The man was crazy and fearless, and Trenika didn't want to jeopardize the lives of those she loved dearly.

And that's when she thought about her grandmother, and a deeper fear settled in her heart. If Trenika could go back for her grandmother she would, but the damage was already done and she needed to go underground. What she did need was a gun of her own, that way if Romell came near her or her daughter, she would take his life.

Now Trenika was angry and decided to snap into the survival training she'd obtained for just this purpose.

It was survival of the fittest.

Trenika had blood in her eyes for the man who wanted to take everything away from her.

Chapter 2

Josh had just stepped out the front door when he heard the first shot rang out. When he looked in the direction of the commotion, he couldn't believe what he saw. A gunman hanging out the window of a drive-by car letting off rounds at the crowd of people standing in front of Grandma Cora's house. He didn't hesitate taking off running in the direction of the house.

When Josh finally made it to his destination, he frowned when he witnessed four people laid out on the sidewalk and in the front yard dead. One of them was little Benji, who took multiple slugs to his face and torso. Another one was Shenita. Then Josh recognized that of Angie slumped in the arms of a hysterical Jhene. There was no question Trenika's best friend was dead. It was a bloody scene and Josh needed to go check on Trenika. He blew past the others, heading straight for the front door of the house.

In passing, Lance was cussing and pacing the front yard while clutching his gun and holding his neck. Obviously one of the bullets had grazed him and he was bleeding profusely. Lance had tears in his eyes as he stared at Benji's dead body.

Upon entering the house, Josh called out for Trenika and went about the home frantically. Then he stepped through the kitchen doorway to see Grandma Cora in the arms of another man sobbing sorrowfully.

"Where is Trenika?" Demanded Josh.

Instantly, the man holding the old lady released her and sneered up at Josh like a vicious hyena. "Who the fuck is you, nigga?"

He advanced on him. "Who the fuck are you?" Josh challenged him.

"No!" Grandma Cora bellowed when she saw the other man make the move to strike out at Josh.

That one blow was all it took to knock Josh out cold. The big man fell hard and hit the floor, banging the side of his head against the corner of the kitchen counter.

Darkness swallowed Josh for sure.

When Josh eventually came to, he opened his eyes and met the tearful but intense gaze of Grandma Cora reaching out to steady him. In her hand was a wet dish towel that she had been pressing against his head injury that was caused by his fall.

"Trenika…?" Josh looked about the kitchen. "Where is she?"

"She's gone, Josh." Said Davida.

"Gone?" Josh felt his heart skip a beat as he thought the worst about what Davida meant.

"What do you mean gone?" He asked in what sounded like a whine.

Grandma Cora told him what happened and about Trenika taking off with Aryanna through the back door.

"Who was that—" he said.

"That was Kaedon, my dear. He doesn't mean you no harm. He was only reacting in regards to Trenika's safety." Grandma Cora cut him off, already knowing what he was asking.

With the shake of his head, Josh winced at the pain it caused and looked up at Lance entering the kitchen. He came to check on his grandmother and acknowledged that the police were on the way. You could actually hear the blaring of police sirens sounding off close by. Lance asked for his sister and Josh told him what was told to him.

"And Kaedon?"

"He went after her," said Davida.

Lance frowned, still holding his neck. Grandma Cora asked him to let her see his wound and he assured her it was just a graze. Then he looked at Davida and told her to not let his grandmother go outside and witness what was out there. He then turned on his heels and ran for the front door to get missing before the police showed up.

Finally, Josh climbed up to his feet and glanced in the direction of the backdoor. "I need to go find her," he said.

"Please?" Said Grandma Cora in desperation. "Please find her and bring her back to us."

He nodded.

"And, Joshua? Don't blame Kaedon, love. Y'all work together and go rescue my babies. Please," cried Grandma Cora as she took him by the hand and looked in his eyes.

Again, he nodded and reluctantly pulled his hand away, then he rushed for the back door.

To find Trenika in a city he knew like the back of his hand, Josh was determined to accomplish his mission. In his line of expertise, tracking people was his specialty. He would find her, even if killing Kaedon in the process to do so. Josh kicked himself mentally for allowing Kaedon to best him the way he did back at the house. He cannot let that slide no matter what Grandma Cora said. Someone had to die for what took place today. It was war.

***

Kaedon wasn't no slack when it came down to hunting down his targets also. But this a whole other entire mission that he was on which was to locate the woman he loved. Kaedon followed the depression of Trenika's footprints through the path into the alleyway where the dirt led to bloody footprints instead. When it was noted that Trenika was hurt, it was all it took for him not to lose his focus.

Finding his family was top priority.

It was life or death, and Kaedon was not going to give up.

He let the bloody prints lead him to the next street over when Kaedon spotted a young kid about twelve riding up the side of the street on a bike. "Yo?" Kaedon waved the kid down and the boy rode up on the bike towards him. "Did you see a female with a little girl come this way, lil' homie?" He asked.

"They went that way." The boy pointed across the street toward two houses where another young kid stood, watching them.

"She went inside one of those houses?"

The boy shook his head and told Kaedon that they had gone between both houses. Kaedon reached in his pocket and peeled off a twenty-dollar bill from his stack of cash. He handed the boy the money and took off in the direction he was given. Kaedon had lost her bloody trail for a moment and found another print inside the next alleyway.

Somewhere nearby, Kaedon heard the police sirens and the roaring of a car engine shooting by up ahead. He hurried towards the commotion and then realized the instant he cleared the alley the commotion was off the trail of bloody footprints that Trenika left behind. Whatever was going on was in the opposite direction from which he was headed.

"C'mon, Kae, you gotta stay on point," he told himself as he continued to follow the tracks of his woman and the existence of his baby girl.

Suddenly Kaedon felt the urge to call Trenika's phone with hopes that she had taken it with her. When he retrieved the phone from his pocket Kaedon hit her number up on speed dial. He longed to hear her voice, to be assured that she was okay. Then, on the seventh ring, the phone was answered and he almost smiled with relief until he heard the wrong voice.

"Kaedon?" It was Jhene, and that was all the reason for him to come to a halt.

"Please tell me my girls are with you, Jhene."

"No." She cried.

He closed his eyes and breathed deeply.

"But I have some bad news. Angie, Benji, and Shenita are dead, brah. And your twin…" Jhene said and Kaedon felt his heart soar with instant dread. "He was shot, too. I'm with him on the way to the hospital in the back of the ambulance. It's not good, Kaedon. We need to find my sista and baby girl. I'm going crazy. I can't do this, brah. Please… I need you to be careful out there," she stressed openly.

"Do you know who the shooter was?"

"No. But I think Lance knows. That's where he's gone to now," she replied.

"Okay. I'm out looking for them right now." Kaedon sped up his pace in following Trenika's trail as he explained to her what he was doing. In the process, he worried about his brother and wanted Jhene to stay with him. Don't leave his side until he was able to come. The last thing he wanted was for his twin brother to die, because that's what was going to really make him snap.

"I'm doing my part," she said.

Kaedon hung up on her and ran the rest of the way which eventually led him to a gas station. Adrenaline surging through him like a tidal wave, he entered the building and followed the trial straight to a restroom door. Kaedon paused to catch his breath and reached for the door handle.

"Nooo," Kaedon growled when he stepped into an empty restroom and saw all the bloody evidence inside.

Chapter 3

Lance cruised past the traffic accident of the car that he knew occupied the shooter that murdered his loved ones. With a screwed face, Lance parked his car nearby so he could join the spectators observing the scene. All he needed was to see who it was that was left slumped in the car. He didn't want to wait to learn the identity of the deceased on the news or in the paper. Lance needed to know now so he would know what his next move would be.

Being careful to not give the authorities reason to question him about the blood on his clothes, Lance pulled over to remove his bloody Polo shirt and checked the trunk for a fresh one. He had parked in the parking lot of a local Burger King fast food joint. Inside the trunk of his Dodge Challenger, Lance always kept something extra handy in case he needed it. He found a crispy white t-shirt in a gym bag and put it on. Lance was in pain, both physically and emotionally, and he wanted to go to war.

After leaving his pistol behind for the moment, Lance made his way toward the crowd of spectators.

The closer he got he plotted on how he was about to make his move. Just one look to identify his man and he was good. He wanted the shooter whom Lance was sure was responsible for the dead person in the car. Once he made it to the crowd, Lance braced himself, then threw caution to the side and burst through the crowd for the car. The whole way there, he screamed that it was his brother in the car. He had made it all the way to the driver door before two police officers snatched him up and pulled him away from the scene. They shoved him back toward the crowd of people standing on the sidewalk, but Lance had already seen what he needed to see.

He played the role of a grieving brother for a minute longer and headed for his car. With a wicked smirk on his face, Lance knew now what his next move was.

Back on the road again he contemplated on going to see his aunt Wanda to deliver the bad news about Benji. She was going to lose her damn mind. Then again, she probably already knew by now and would demand that he find her son's killer. His auntie would set her Christian morals aside to make it clear that she wanted her son's killer dealt with accordingly. So, Lance decided to go ahead and move forward with his next plan of attack.

"Hello?" The voice picked up

"Gator, it's me. L-Dawg," said Lance, with Boosie Badazz playing in the background. "I need your help on something. You remember the lil' nigga who pulled that move on Rico and 'em a few months back about a stolen car?"

"The shit at the liquor store?"

"Yeah."

"I remember. What about it? The lil' fool that did that is from Magnolia Projects," said Gator.

"What's his name, brah?"

It took Gator a minute to remember the name. "Boon...? Bang...? Bam! Yeah, that's the one. He's supposed to be Boss Hog's lil' protege, a lil' bad muthafucker. Him and the young nigga Mack is real close," Gator said knowledgeably, obviously in the middle of a smoke session by the strained voice he was using from a throat full of weed smoke.

The instant Gator said the name Boss Hog it was confirmed what Lance needed to do. This was another street nigga that Lance had recently bumped heads with regarding

Benji's involvement with making moves on his turf. The issue was that Benji had been seeing some bitch out Boss Hog's hood and was also pushing his product there. When Boss Hog learned of this, he sent a couple of goons after Benji and got one dead goon back. But that was before Boss Hog found out that Benji was Lance's cousin and the two gangstaz called a truce. Boss Hog gave him his word that no further incident would occur concerning the matter.

"A'ight, my nigga. Thanks." Lance replied.

"You need me to pull up or what?" Said Gator, always ready to shed some blood.

Lance told him no, and then he ended the call, promising Gator that he would get back with him. Next, he began plotting on how he was going to deal with Boss Hog because those bullets had been meant for him initially; the shooter was trying to take him out first. Lance didn't believe in the coincidence that if Bam was involved, that he was part of the issue where Benji's life was in danger. To get to Benji you had to kill Lance, but Benji still ended up being murdered anyway, and now Boss Hog and whoever else behind him must answer to that.

"No mercy," Lance hissed like a venomous snake as he pulled up into the entrance of an auto parts store. Once he stole himself a car, it was on to another murder scene.

There would be no mercy indeed.

Boss Hog had to die.

Somebody.

***

When the forest green Mazda CX-30 pulled up outside the local Super Walmart and parked out front before the entrance, Trenika hurried out and deposited Aryanna in the back and climbed up front with Cindy Adams. She figured if there was anybody that Romell wouldn't expect her to be with, it would be the lawyer that she met on the plane. It took

Trenika awhile to remember the lawyer's name, but after looking through the city's phone book for the connection, she found it. She remembered the lawyer saying that she had her own firm downtown and searched for her there.

When Trenika called the lawyer from a payphone and said that she was in trouble, Cindy didn't hesitate coming to her rescue. Trenika was so grateful for the woman's loyalty that she tearfully kissed her cheek and hugged her.

"Please get me away from here, Cindy. I don't wanna be out like this," said Trenika, having gone through pure hell after running away from home once again.

"No problem." Cindy put the truck in gear and they were on the move. In her peripheral she noticed that Trenika's hair was in disarray, she wasn't properly dressed for an outing, and she was wearing a pair of boots that didn't go with the wife beater and pajama bottoms she had on. Something told her that whatever she was going through, Trenika was so scared of it that she didn't care about her appearance.

Trenika turned back to look at Aryanna and rubbed her little scrawny leg reassuringly. She offered her daughter a weak smile and baby girl just looked at her with a straight face.

"Are you okay, baby girl?"

"I want daddy," Aryanna replied.

"What happened, Trenika? I'm sorry for whatever's going on with you, but I need to know where I stand in all this. Will you need any legal representation?" Asked Cindy.

"Maybe after I find the bastard and put a stop to him once and for all." Trenika stared out her side window at the passing traffic, and with a heavy sigh she told Cindy everything. It wouldn't be right to involve the lawyer and not tell her all about the monster she called Romell.

As Cindy listened to the horrific details of Trenika's situation, her own past afflictions came rushing back to her. Her stepmom had died from AIDS after running off with another man that wasn't her father. It led her father to deal with his losing a second wife at the bottom of whiskey bottles. The man drank himself to death while cursing Cindy's stepmom all the way there.

After growing up without her father and mother since her junior year in high school, Cindy's aunt Paula was there to guide her through life and its many obstacles.

But here it was Trenika having been betrayed by the man she once loved and who had ruined her life with H.I.V. Cindy felt her pain. The woman literally watched her father die slowly as a result of his wife stepping out on him with another man who tainted her life with the deadly virus.

Could this be God's way of reminding Cindy of her father's situation where she couldn't help him, but now she could finally redeem herself by helping Trenika?

When it was all said and done, Cindy had taken Trenika and her daughter to her own home. It was a gated community residence with strict security that Cindy doubted anyone of Romell's caliber could breach without consequences. She welcomed them into her home to which she shared with her amazing collie, Rufus Lee. Upon entering the big townhouse Aryanna was immediately taken with the dog and forgot all about her troubles.

"Thank you again, Cindy. I wouldn't have called if I'd known you couldn't help us," said Trenika, following the woman into the bright lit kitchen.

"You've chosen wisely," Cindy replied. She proceeded to pour them both a glass of wine to calm their nerves. "I also have a few friends who are cops that could look into that situation at your grandmother's house."

"Please do that for me, Cindy. I need to know if my family and friends are all okay." Trenika had a bad feeling that whatever took place at her grandmother's house didn't end well. She could still hear the gunshots and the screams in her head. Both were sounds of death and horror.

"Let me get right to it for you," said Cindy after downing what's left of the contents in her glass. "Make yourself at home, Trenika. The bathroom is down the hall on the left. I'll be just a minute," she told her before hurrying off out the kitchen.

Trenika sat the glass of wine down and leaned forward to put her head onto her arm. She wanted to leave New Orleans and go back home. But she was afraid that Romell would hunt her all the way back there as well. He damn sure found her in Quincy after four years. He wouldn't stop until he finds her for good.

Trenika lifted up her head with a start. "I thought…" she gave off a ponderous expression. "What is he doing out right now? Didn't he have nine months left to do?" She said.

"Mommy, who are you talking to?" Aryanna entered the kitchen with Rufus Lee tagging along.

Snapping out of her daze, Trenika turned to look at her daughter and said, "I was just thinking out loud, baby girl. Mommy has a lot on her mind right now."

"I keep telling you, mommy." Aryanna climbed up onto the stool next to her mother. "Daddy will make everything right. All you gotta do is call him. If you need a hero…"

"Daddy is your hero." Trenika finished the saying that Kaedon always said to baby girl to keep her mind at ease. She didn't doubt that one bit and Kaedon was probably worried sick about them both. She would love to call Kaedon and tell him to come get them, but Trenika's fear of Romell watching him or having intel on any communication technology-wise. Romell had always considered himself tech-savvy, and there's no telling what all he had learned while incarcerated.

One had to seriously beware of someone like Romell and his hunger for revenge.

He was dangerous.

The nigga could not be trusted. Plus, he was dying too, so he had no regards on life at all.

Chapter 4

The clerk behind the counter of the gas station told Kaedon everything she knew concerning the incident with Trenika and Aryanna. When he followed the bloody steps all the way to the restroom of the gas station, Kaedon knew for sure he had found his girls. But all hopes failed when he opened the door and found it empty.

Kaedon approached the female clerk and wasn't satisfied with what he was told. So, he told the clerk, who was a twenty-something black woman named Eboni, that he needed to review the video footage of their existence. The clerk wasn't having it until Kaedon gave her that murderous glare that made her shudder.

In the back, reviewing the video footage by himself, Kaedon was eventually disturbed by the sudden commotion going on out front. He didn't really recognize Josh's voice, but when he heard Eboni explaining the situation concerning Trenika, he stopped what he was doing. Then he moved over to the door to the manager's office and looked out to see Josh standing there. Remembering what he did to the nigga back at the house made Kaedon want to put a stop to him for good. But he also thought about Grandma Cora's warnings and her explanation who Josh was and what role he played in the matter. Seeing the man now up front questioning the clerk about Trenika and baby girl really was doing something to his mental. Before it was all said and done Kaedon believed he would end up killing Josh because he was becoming a real problem.

There was only one hero in their lives and Kaedon was determined to uphold that role.

The video showed Trenika exiting the restroom and approached the front counter. In the process, Aryanna exited the restroom and began looking around for something. Then baby girl found what she was looking for, which was bandages and medicated creams and such, to which she stuffed in her shirt and reentered the restroom. It was then that Kaedon witnessed just how slick and swift his five-year-old daughter actually was. His heart swelled up with pride to see Aryanna making the proper moves to see that her mother had what she needed to take care of herself.

After what seemed like forever, Trenika exited the restroom for the second time along with baby girl and hurried out of the building going west towards downtown. That's what Kaedon needed to see and left out the manager's office with a new purpose.

Having forgotten all about Josh being the thorn in his side, Kaedon exited the gas station right into the nigga's path. Josh had been on the phone talking to someone when Kaedon literally stepped around him and headed westbound along Main Street. When Josh called after him, he just kept right on pushing forward. Dealing with the man was the last thing Kaedon needed, but if Josh pushed him then there would be hell to pay.

"You're not the only one that loves her and wants to see her back home safe, Kaedon," said Josh.

At hearing those words Kaedon halted and looked over his shoulder at the man. "I'm warning you, dawg, stay away from my family if you know what's good for you. I got this, nigga."

"Is that a threat, Kaedon?"

"It's all that." Kaedon glared in his direction.

"I'ma chalk that shit up as your emotions talking, but I don't take threats too kindly. I've known Tee since we were kids, Kaedon, so I'm just as obligated to find her and her daughter as you are. I don't wanna beef with you, I just want to find my friend. Our best plan of action is that we work together, Kaedon. I'm from here, you're not, and I can help you find her," said Josh with reason, still not liking the look he was getting from the other man.

Kaedon was also a man of reason when he wanted to, and he had already wasted too much time talking to this nigga. Trenika was at least fifteen or twenty minutes ahead from the timeline he got from the video footage.

Right then a silver Jaguar pulled up and came to rest next to Josh. Behind the wheel was a pretty brown skin chick with a cell phone to her ear.

"Let's go, cuz! I just got word they saw Tee and her daughter over at the Super Walmart up the street," said the female behind the wheel of the car.

"What do you say, Kaedon? Time is of the essence." Josh met the furious gaze of the other man.

Hesitantly, Kaedon said, "When this shit is all over, dawg, me and you gotta get some straightening."

"I'm down with that," said Josh. "When it's over, we gotta get out back somewhere and shoot me a fair fight."

"Say no more." Kaedon nodded.

A moment later Josh hopped in the passenger seat of the Jag and Kaedon got in behind him. Once they were in traffic, Kaedon smirked deviously to himself at the critical situation the nigga had put himself in. If Kaedon was on some other shit, he could snap Josh's neck from behind with no problem. The nigga was a sitting duck right now without knowing that he had a real deal killer in his proximity.

It took them a few minutes to reach the Walmart shopping center where Josh's cousin, Shelia's homegirl Sophia, was waiting on them outside the building. Sophia was an older female around Trenika's age and as big as a cow. When the

Jag pulled up on the set Sophia wobbled her fat ass over to the car in her blue Walmart uniform apron on.

"Where is she?" Shelia wanted to know.

Kaedon was climbing out of the car when Sophia said Trenika and baby girl left with some white female in a green SUV. He looked at the fat chick and frowned.

"Any idea what type of SUV it was?" Asked Josh.

"Nope," said Sophia. "I don't know."

That's when Kaedon asked her was it possible that she could review the store's video footage. "It's worth a try," he said.

"I might can be able to do that, though. Monica is the supervisor today and she'll let me do it for Trenika."

"Let's go make sure," Kaedon said and shut the passenger door closed. "Getting the make of the truck would narrow it down to just who it might be," he added, looking at Josh before following Sophia's wide booty into the store. Knowing his woman like he does, Trenika wouldn't go with anyone she knew. One would easily detect her whereabouts.

***

After killing Bam and catching Ghost, Romell hit the side streets on foot until he ducked off into a local pawn shop. He needed to get off the scene for now until Beno came to scoop him up. Beno was his baby mama Layla's baby brother, the same bitch whose life he had destroyed too. But being that Layla had been fucking out of both pants legs, he had a way of making her believe that she had given the virus to him instead of the other way around.

Romell was a master manipulator and had a thing for playing on people's weaknesses when dealing with him. He was a poet, a man of charming words and good at pretending. When he kicked in Layla's door and blamed her for giving him H.I.V., he threatened to kill her while declaring his love for her at the same time. He made her feel so bad that Layla was contemplating committing suicide.

Romell, being the manipulator that he was, convinced Layla that they still could have a life together. He made her stop whoring around and focused all her energy on pleasing him only. So much so that she bore him a little boy named Roman Dontarious and he was four years old and surprisingly healthy without the virus. Layla was so gullible, and Romell used it to his benefit. The whole time he was down, it was Layla who had been his backbone.

She turned out to be a loyal rider and Romell was convinced that she was worth calling wifey.

The nigga was really sick in the head, and he knew one day that it would come back on him. But until then he planned to milk his game for as long as he could.

Like with Bam for example, Romell learned of the situation regarding Benji killing his homeboy when Boss Hog sent his killaz after him. Romell saw a pawn in using Bam as the scapegoat if all else failed. Apparently, fate decided that Lance should stay amongst the land of the living. But not without putting the pieces together and used Bam's murder in connection to what transpired between him and Boss Hog's truce. Romell knew how niggas like Lance thought on such matters, which is why he wasn't worried about repercussions against him.

"I'm a beast with this shit," Romell said to himself as he dwelt on his situation.

Before long Trenika would alert them all that it was him that pulled the trigger, that's if she hadn't let the cat out of the bag already. And if she had spilled the beans then he had a mean trick for all of them.

After waiting about fifteen minutes and purchasing a few things he found in the pawn shop, Beno pulled up in his old BMW 850 bumping some Lil' Durk. Romell exited the pawn shop and directed Beno to a secluded spot near a mechanic garage on a back street inside an alley. There he retrieved the Mac .90 he had hid behind a big steel dumpster.

"What the fuck is that, Romell?" Beno asked when Romell got into the car with the big gun. He was no stranger to such things, but Beno wasn't no gangsta either.

Romell ignored his question and told him to take him to the house. He would wait until nightfall to come back out and create more havoc. What happened earlier was just a spur of the moment, although he'd known since the day before that Trenika was back home this morning when he saw another man proposing to her. It didn't sit well with him, and he just wanted to strike out at somebody.

Tonight, he was going to really show his fangs.

That dawg in him was hungry for blood.

Been hungry for a very long time.

"I need a favor from you, Beno, but you must give me your word that you won't mention this to no one," Romell said and glanced over in his direction.

"C'mon, my nigga. You're not riding with me if you didn't trust me to handle my business. I know all about what went down over in the Seventh Ward. There's no doubt in my mind you were behind that, but only because I know you are home. It does not take a rocket scientist to figure it out after what happened with your own people. I know what's going on, Romell; I'm out there in those streets for real," said Beno.

Romell shrugged. "I need you to slide over there and see what's the talk about. I need some confirmation."

"I got you," Beno gave his word. "I know what to do."

About all the other shit Beno said a minute ago, Romell could not refute that. He was right in every aspect of the sense of knowledge Romell's past afflictions. Soon the world will know his name and he would become legend. And when it was his time to go, he would have created so much destruction that it would take many years to come back from.

Chapter 5

The stolen car was a blue Mitsubishi Gallant with dark tinted windows. Lance took the car from a nearby doctor's office instead of the auto parts store where his timeline would be short. At last, at a doctor's office, the stretch of time would be longer and enough opportunity to do what he needed to do.

When that was done, Lance went over to the trap house he operated and equipped himself with a weapon he only used once before. It was a .30-caliber Browning air-cooled machine gun that he purchased off the black market a year ago. The last time he was in possession of the gun it scared him with all the damage it created. He loaded the gun into a blanket and told his man, Hawk, to come roll with him.

Hawk was a twenty-five-year-old goon whom Lance had known for quite some time now having earned himself the reputation of a fearless hooter, he earned himself a position working as a guard over Lance's trap house. Today he needed someone he could trust to keep his mouth shut. Not saying that the other two workers, Spud and Cam, were not trustworthy, he just felt more secure with Hawk.

Leaving the other two workers to hold the fort down at the trap house, Lance and Hawk loaded into the stolen car and headed out to the 'Nolia.

"So, what's the move, soldier?" asked Hawk. The name was given to him because he indeed looked like a bird. And the characteristics of him were humility, soft-spoken, anti-social, and very loyal to those who loyal to him.

Lance told him about what went down at the house and about losing Benji in the process. This seemed to anger Hawk because he and Benji were friends. It was Benji who had actually convinced him to come aboard and take the security position at the trap house.

"I've been wanting to give that bitch nigga Boss Hog the business," said Hawk.

"Well, his day has come," said Lance.

"Lemme give it to him, soldier," Hawk said from behind the wheel of the car. "Go see about your family and leave him to me. I know this is a personal issue with you regarding him but with me —"

"Save all that shit, my nigga." Lance unwrapped the big gun of the blanket and tossed the blanket in the back. "Boss Hog is mine," he said.

The 'Nolia territory was empty of Boss Hog's presence, and so they rode all over the city looking for him. It was known that Boss Hog, who headed his own drug empire and never showed face unless it was necessary, was not likely to be discovered in just any place. Although he was a big player in the streets with his own squad, he still had his share of enemies, and killing him could grant one abundant glory. Lane was one of a few gangstas who stood up to Boss Hog and didn't end up in a body bag. But that was because Boss Hog knew him to be a stand-up guy, and that he was only acting in defense of his cousin. If Boss Hog had ever heard of Lance doing shady business or thought he was a snake, then their differences would have gone another way a few months ago. But from one thorough gangsta to another, a truce was what had been more appropriate between the two of them. Respect was due then, but now it was not about that. After what happened today made Lance believe that Boss Hog didn't have control on his own men. Bam was one of his own, and whoever killed Bam to prevent him from giving them up, Boss Hog had to be aware of it.

And if he didn't then Lance was about to make him wish Bam had never been a part of his team.

All it took was for one apple to spoil the bunch.

Twenty-two minutes of searching for the big man, Boss Hog was found occupying a five-star diner eating breakfast with his four goons. But to Lance's surprise, the nigga's carelessness with sitting near a big window overlooking the view of a national park across the lot was what he was about to use to his advantage.

"Checkmate," muttered Lance when he unlocked the safety of the gun and then was given a red bandana and a fitted cap from Hawk. "That's why I fuck's with you, my nigga. You're always on point," he replied as he disguised himself with the items he was given.

"You were about to do some suicidal shit just now," Hawk responded to his statement.

Without another word, Lance took a deep breath and bolted from the car with the monster in his hand. He shot across the parking lot ducking low as he came up on Boss Hog's blind side. Lance upped his weapon as he stepped in front of the big window and let that muthafucker loose.

"Pussy muthafuckerz!" Lance bellowed as the machine gun spat fire and filled Boss Hog and his crew up with hot lead. Blood and glass were splattered everywhere.

When the car pulled up behind Lance, he heard Hawk call out to him and he jumped in immediately. The car sped away from the scene. Lance hollered like a madman. He had finally slain the big bag giant.

But little did he know, the blood he had just spilled was about to set the city on fire.

***

Cindy entered the living room where Trenika and Aryana were huddled together on the sofa watching some animated movie called Strange World. When Trenika looked up at her entry Cindy beckoned her over with a head nod.

Moments later the two women met back up in the kitchen. The look Trenika saw on the lawyer's face wasn't good. Right then Trenika knew she was about to learn some very disturbing news. Her heart began racing like crazy when Cindy handed her a sticky note across the countertop of the island.

"I'm sorry, Trenika. My resource said three were actually killed and those are their names. Two more were also shot and are in critical condition. Their names are at the very bottom. However…" Cindy paused the instant she saw silent tears begin streaming down Trenika's face as she stared down at the names on the sticky note. "The getaway vehicle was also located a few blocks away from the scene with its driver dead behind the wheel."

Shenita. Angei. Benji. Those three names of her loved ones who died today and it left Trenika feeling devastated. Never in her life would she ever expect something like this would happen. Then with Zamon being shot too, Trenika could just imagine what Kaedon was going through at that moment. And Clifford Hayes, he was just an older neighborhood friend who lived in the house next door to her grandmother. All these people Trenika loved and respected. They were all dead because of her.

"Romell?" Trenika finally looked up at the lawyer, this time her eyes filled with pure hatred.

"He was released four days ago with good gain time credited. His day for day ends in nine months early next year, but due to his good behavior he was released early. Are you sure this is the guy you saw, Trenika?" Cindy asked.

Trenika shot her a dark glare for asking such a question. "Cindy?"

The white lawyer tossed her hands up in surrender. "I'm just trying to be certain because I can have my guys put an APB out on him. Do you know anyone by the name of Wayne Foye?"

"No. Who is he?"

"He's the dead driver of the getaway vehicle."

Whoever he was, Trenika was sure her brother Lance would figure it out. She didn't want to say too much which could hinder her brother's mission to avenge the deaths of his loved ones. By now Lance was probably out there with Kaedon fucking some shit up. If those two had teamed up then the streets of New Orleans were in some serious trouble.

"What are your thoughts right now, Trenika?" Cindy broke her out of her thought process.

"Revenge." Trenika admitted.

Shaking her head, Cindy made her way around the island to come stand next to the other woman. Feeling obligated to do so, she told Trenika about the importance of letting the authorities deal with the situation. That she had a daughter to protect and that she needed to think smartly, because all it takes is one bad decision and everything could go up in smoke.

"It's too late for that," Trenika replied.

"It's never too late, honey. You still have your whole life ahead of you with a beautiful little girl that needs you."

"Can I use your phone?" Trenika wasn't hearing her at that moment.

Reluctantly, the lawyer woman nodded and left the kitchen to go retrieve her cellphone. In the process, Trenika moved over to the doorway of the kitchen to look at her daughter. The collie, Rufus Lee, had taken her place on the sofa next to Aryanna. Just looking at her precious daughter really did remind her how important it was to keep her safe from harm.

Trenika would die protecting her daughter. She wondered if Cindy had a gun and would let her use it for the time being. She could never be too careful in a situation like this.

Cindy returned with her iPhone 10 and Trenika blocked the number before calling Kaedon's phone. She needed to hear his voice to ensure her love to him and that she was safe. She needed Kaedon to know who was responsible.

"Hello?" Kaedon answered on the second ring.

A lone tear fell from her eyes at hearing the voice of the man that just proposed his love for her for dear life. "It's me, Kae," she replied emotionally.

"Baby, where are you and baby girl? I'll come get y'all and take you home. I need you. I love you... Where are you?" Kaedon sounded so desperate that it broke her heart. There was no mistaking the love and fear she also heard in his voice.

Trenika said, "It was Romell."

A momentary silence hung in the air between them.

"You know this for a fact?" He asked.

Trenika wished she was standing in front of Kaedon or else he wouldn't have said those six words. He would have witnessed the truth in her eyes like he'd done many times before.

She told him what she saw, which was the sole reason she denied his proposal. "But I'm safe though, Kae. Me and baby girl are where no one would find us."

"Where is that? I'll come straight there to you."

"I can't," she said.

"Why not?"

"Just take care of business and make sure you put that dog down once and for all. Okay? Trust me, baby. I got us. We are safe here."

"But you're safer with me," he said evenly.

"I'm not, Kaedon. I'm sorry. He knows who you are now and there's no tellin' if he's watching you right now or not. Then again, you could expect that he is and you don't wanna lead that monster straight to me. So do you and know that me and baby girl are counting on you."

"Trenika?" He called out to her. "Bae?"

"Yeah?" She closed her eyes and willed her heart to be still.

"I love you. It's done." He said.

"I know," she said. Then she disconnected the call with hopes that Kaedon took her not saying that she loved him back as motivation to hear her say it in person. There was a lot she wanted to say but she needed him to focus on the mission accordingly. Then she hollered for Cindy who appeared in the kitchen doorway a moment later.

"Did you hear what else happened?" Cindy asked.

"I don't know what you're talkin' about, Cindy. What else has happened?" Asked Trenika

All the lawyer could do was look at her and shake her head sadly. "Follow me," she said, leading her way to her home office.

Chapter 6

Jhene was sitting in the waiting room of the city hospital looking quite disturbed. Her clothes were filthy with Angie's blood and Zamon's, whom she was waiting to see how his surgery was going. He had been shot twice, once in the stomach and another in the right shoulder. Clifford had taken a slug to the back of his thigh. Jhene had been so scared that she thought she would go into a panic attack.

When they arrived at the hospital two detectives were already there waiting to get her statement. They had just left her five minutes ago after trying to force her to tell them something she didn't know about.

Jhene was emotionally exhausted from all the bullshit.

She was scared to death. Scared for her best friend and what all this could mean to her. Last time Trenika had run away when things got too drastic, now she might have done it again and never to return this time. Losing her sister from another mother was already hard on all of them. With Angie getting killed in the process just might do Trenika in for good.

Just thinking about her two friends and Benji and what all this shit could pose, it left Jhene in tears again. She cried for her loved ones, and it hurt badly.

"Jhene!"

Jhene looked up at someone calling her name and saw Davida rushing in her direction. At the sight of her friend her tears came down in thick streams.

Behind Davida was Boogie, a well-known gangsta who had a reputation for bodying niggas and cracking skulls. This was Shenita's big brother, the very same nigga that was said to have ties with the mob.

Davida made her way over to her childhood friend and gathered her into her embrace. Together they cried for their dead friends, leaving Boogie to look on in deep grief.

A minute later Kaedon and Josh exited the elevator and headed directly for the women. When Boogie saw the two men coming his way with grim expressions, he moved his hand towards the pistol he had tucked at his waist beneath his jacket. Kaedon eyes him suspiciously and steps up to come to a halt in front of the two devastated sisters.

"Kaedon," said Davida, wiping her face and rising up to her feet to face Kaedon. She reached out and took his hand into her own. "You learned anything yet about our girl?"

"I just spoke with her on the way here," he answered and Jhene perked up at his words.

"Where is she? Why isn't she here with us?" Jhene asked.

"Because she's too afraid to be," Kaedon said. He then told them what he knew of Trenika and Aryanna's situation, while making a point of investigating her last time being seen at Wal-Mart. He gave them the short version of how he came about tracking her journey and bumping into Josh on the way.

Josh then told them about the white woman and the green SUV to which they now knew was a Mazda.

"Sounds familiar," said Boogie, tall and slender built with a low-cut temp fade. He had been watching Kaedon hand, recognizing a real gangsta and wondering where he came from. "Do you know what this white lady actually looks like?"

"We have no description of her other than her hair being of a reddish tint," said Josh.

Boogie scratched his beard with a ponderous expression as though he was trying to figure out something.

"Fuck this. How bad is my brother?" Kaedon couldn't wait to get to this point in the conversion. He moved over to a distraught Jhene and sat down beside her. He was grateful for her being there for his twin the way she did.

She told him what she knew, and Kaedon looked in the direction of where he expected the operation room to be.

"Don't," said Josh laying his hand on Kaedon's shoulder. "Let them do their jobs. He's with some of the best surgeons in the whole country working to save him." He added.

"He's right, Kaedon. I know this for a fact because I worked here for six years. I still have a few favors owed to me in here so I'll go see what I can find out." Davida stood her plumped frame up to her feet and left them to go in search of her acquainted associates.

Pulling out his cellphone, Kaedon contemplated calling Zamon's cell phone somehow and do it that way.

As he was contemplating his next move, an idea came to mind in regards to Romell's situation. If Lance and Benji had killed off all Romell's people, there had to be someone he trusted to come home to. Whoever that was he intended to find out and very soon.

He called Ciera to check up on her first.

Then he put his plan in motion.

***

Layla Miller was in the living room of her house undoing her micro braids while humming to some slow jams outpouring from her stereo sound system. She paused briefly at the booming vibrations of Beno's car sound system as it pulled around the back of her house.

Minutes later the patio door opened, and Romell entered the house calling out to her and his son. Layla smiled and got up to go meet her man. He entered the room carrying a shopping bag and handed it to her with a kiss placed upon her luscious lips.

37

"What is this, baby?" Layla asked as she proceeded to look inside the bag.

Romell grinned broadly when she squealed gleefully and did some type of excited tap dance in her bare feet as she extracted her gift from the bag. It was a pair of Versace earrings that she'd been desiring to have. He had remembered the same exact ones and knew getting them would make her happy as ever.

"I love you so much, baby. Thank you!" Layla threw her shapely arms around his neck and kissed him.

All Romell could do was smile proudly. "Where's Roman at?"

He inquired about his son.

"His grandmama came to get him and took him with her. We are supposed to meet back up after the Labor Day parade and have dinner together." Layla glanced back down at the second shopping bag Romell had in his hand. "You got him another pair of shoes? He's got like ten pairs already, Rome," she said.

"Not this time," he told her.

"What you got him this time then, Santa Claus?"

"Touch your nose." He smirked.

She slapped him playfully on the arm and allowed him to kiss her again before turning around to go take the shopping bag into their son's bedroom.

When Romell turned his back Layla's expression transformed into a look of weariness. She wondered if her man was aware that he had specs of blood on his Gucci shirt. He didn't appear as though he was hurt or anything, which could mean that the blood belonged to someone else. And if indeed it does belong to someone else then her fears have come to reality.

Before Romell was incarcerated, he had told her all about the deaths of his loved ones. He didn't give any specific names as to who murdered his family, only that one day he will pay back those who were responsible. Layla knew it was a heavy weight on her man's shoulders, a burden that left him awake at night. Romell promised he wouldn't rest until he avenged the deaths of those he once cared for deeply.

And that's what scared her at that moment, figuring Romell having begun his retaliation that just might come back and haunt them all.

Praying that she was wrong by his actions, Layla headed down the hallway to be with her man. She was not going to question him about what she detected. She was not going to give up hope that Romell would build them a better life. Layla just wanted to go please her man and let him know that she was forever there for him.

She found Romell in the shower a minute later to which she stripped down to nothing and joined him. In the shower, Layla took up the sponge and washed his back and kissed the back of his neck. When Romell turned around to face her his dick was hard as a rock. She gave him that sultry look of hers and reached out to take ahold of his tool and stroked it back and forth.

"You know where I want it at," Romell told her as he reached to caress her Double Ds softly.

"It's yours, daddy." Layla turned her back to him and cocked her right leg up onto the ledge of the bathtub. Reaching a hand behind her to take possession of his dick again, Layla rubbed its head against the opening of her asshole.

"Oohhh shit!" Romell bit his bottom lip when Layla goaded him to push slowly into her back passage. Her asshole was tight like a glove, until it eventually opened up where he could do his thing without causing too much pain.

Layla moaned in pleasure as he plunged into her with long slow strokes that made her eyes roll to the back of her head in satisfaction.

"Stop bullshittin' and give me that pound game," said Layla looking back over her shoulder at him. "I want you to power drive this ass, baby." She pleaded.

You didn't have to tell him twice. Romell gripped both hands onto her thick waist and got busy. Sawing in and out of her ass and slapping her ass cheeks in the process, Romell gave her that thug passion.

"That's what I'm talkin' about, Rome! Get it! Get it how you like it, baby!" Layla pushed back against him, meeting him stroke for stroke and screaming in ecstasy.

He was doing his thing for the next ten minutes and exploded into her. Romell growled and pulled her back against him spent.

"Damn," was all he could say.

Afterwards Layla wiped his dick lean and sent him on his way. Layla waited until he left the bathroom before she pressed her head against the wall and cried. She loved her man but wasn't happy. She was scared. All she wanted was to live free and be happy. But she couldn't because she was too busy worrying whether she would live or die now that Romell has sought out revenge.

Chapter 7

The front door opened suddenly, and Ciera froze when she saw Alex Junior. playing with his PSP handheld game. Malik and Tyquan pushed her aside to enter the house at the prospect of seeing Kaedon, Trenika, and Aryanna. But both boys came to a sudden halt at the sight of Alex Junior and asked who he was.

Ciera shut the door behind her and entered further into the house just as another woman exited from the kitchen along with a young teenage girl.

"Ciera," said the woman as she approached her.

"Do I know you?" Ciera asked.

"No. But I'm Jourdan, this is AJ and Donecia, and my husband Al is asleep right now. You're Kaedon's big sister, and someone whom Trenika adores immensely. I'm a friend of Trenika, she's the one who welcomed us into her home," said Jourdan.

"And where is she now?" Ciera asked.

"In New Orleans," she answered

New Orleans? thought Ciera as she watched Malik approach Alex Junior, interested in the video game he was playing. The boy was a game fanatic too and wanted to go over and make friends with him.

Ciera ignored the outstretched hand the woman offered and said, "And Kaedon?"

Before she could answer there was a knock at the front door that caused Jourdan to flinch. Instinctively, Ciera noticed the dreaded look on the woman's face and the alertness in her eyes. Suddenly the knock on the front door spooked her and Ciera wondered what all that was about.

"Ciera?" Jourdan reached out to take her arm when she made an attempt to turn for the door. "Please. There's something I must tell you before you go open that front door. It's a matter of life or death, she said.

Snatching away from her grasp, Ciera looked up at the strange woman and said, "What do you mean life or death?"

"We're in danger," she said with pleading eyes and beckoning for her children to come near.

Whoever was at the front door went for another round of knocking but with more emphasis this time. A man's voice called out to them announcing that he was with the FBI and he just wanted to talk to them. At the mention of the FBI Ciera looked from the direction of the door back over at Jourdan. She told the woman to start talking and do it fast, making it clear that she didn't appreciate her having the FBI at her brother's front door.

Jourdan rattled off the reason for which she was standing where she was right now. It was as if she had rehearsed what she was delivering in case someone asked.

Before allowing the woman to finish Ciera shooed her off and went to go answer the door. In the process, she removed her blouse to make it look like she had been busy getting undressed when they came calling.

Behind her she heard Jourdan ushering her children out of the front room down the hallway. The woman was scared to death and if what she said was real, then she had good damn reason to be.

At the door Ciera snatched it open and glared coldly at the surprisingly good-looking older black guy standing on the doorstep. She wanted to really size him up but had to snap into her role of an angry woman. The man was taken aback by her own beauty and coming to the door shirtless with just her bra on.

"Do you mind?" She snapped at him. "I'm just gettin' in and trying to relax, and here you are beating the damn door down like you don't have no sense. Now what the hell do you want?" Ciera replied with an attitude.

The man produced his FBI credentials and introduced himself as Agent Amos McNair, standing there in his windbreaker and casual attire. "Are you the owner of this residence, ma'am?" He asked her.

"No, I am not. The house belongs to my brother and his family. They are out of town right now and I've just arrived from out of town with my children," she said.

"And you're arriving from where exactly?" He asked.

"From Quincy, Florida. What is all these questions about, Agent McNair?" Ciera looked at him perplexed.

Trying his best to keep from staring at her breasts, the man told her that he was following up on an incident that occurred next door involving a murder. "And I was just curious to who you were and maybe get a statement."

"I don't know anything about no murder. Like I said, I just got in, sir."

"Duly noted, ma'am. And your name is?"

"Ciera Crawford."

He nodded and told her how much he appreciated her help, then he handed her his card and told her to give him a call if she learned anything regarding the investigation.

Ciera slammed the door in his face and re-entered the family room where she retrieved her phone to call her brother. She wasn't just going to take Jourdan's word for it, she needed to hear it from someone she trusted.

Right at that moment Jourdan came from down the hallway with her own phone in hand. She extended it towards Ciera and told her that Trenika was already on the phone. Ciera took the phone while regarding the woman with caution.

"Hello?"

"She's alright, Cee Cee. It's okay. I just heard about what took place next door. It's all just so crazy, sister. I didn't think it would go this far," said Trenika.

"Well, it did, and somebody's dead." Ciera pointed out.

"It's no different from here too, Cee Cee." Then Trenika told her all about what was happening in New Orleans with all the killings there too.

Ciera gasped in dread at the knowledge of Kaedon being involved and what her brother might be going through. This was not what she expected to learn when she came to Atlanta. She wanted to be with her brother and his family and maybe go to the Labor Day parade and hang out. Here she was surrounded by a strange family and a murder investigation. Her whole day has been spoiled with bullshit.

"If it ain't one thang it's another," said Ciera.

Trenika released a deep sigh. "Who you're tellin'," she said.

***

Later that evening Kaedon stood at his brother's bedside staring down at him in deep thought. Zamon had made it out of surgery successfully, but he was still in bad condition. The slug to his stomach hadn't hit any major organs, but it did travel through and slammed against his spinal cord. Zamon was reportedly paralyzed from the waist down due to the damage the bullet did to his vertebrate. But more tests had to be done to determine whether he had a chance of recovering from it or not.

Kaedon felt like he was losing his twin brother already and they just began to get fully acquainted.

By this time tomorrow Zamon's wife and newborn child would be at his bedside. By then Kaedon planned to be knee deep in the streets looking for Romell. After confiding in Lance about what Trenika told him earlier, Kaedon shared with the other gangsta his idea on the possibility of where he could probably locate Romell.

Lance also put a $50,000 hit on Romell's head and had put the ticket in through all the underground channels. Dead or alive, Romell had to get dealt with accordingly.

When Kaedon learned of the hit, he phoned Lance and told him how bad of an idea that was. At least right now what with the plan of action that Kaedon had in mind.

"Before any inmate is released from prison they must produce a standard resident address," Kaedon had told him earlier. "We got to find out what that address was. Plus, we need to find somebody behind the wall who was close enough to Romell for him to trust with information. Once we get that info then we can utilize it to find that muthafucker. And when we find him, we're gonna make his ass bleed," he had vowed.

So, putting a $50,000 hit on Romell might give him reason to run. They needed him under the impression that he was safe being invisible. His best bet was to stay underground during the daytime, because just as soon as he slipped up, he was a dead man. It was conceivable that after what took place with Romell several years ago, he would feel safer coming out at nighttime now. Perhaps that was Romell's plan to remain inconspicuous and separate from anybody who could identify him and his whereabouts.

Kaedon's anxious thoughts were interrupted when a knock sounded off at the door and Grandma Cora entered the room. When he met the old woman's gaze Kaedon automatically knew why she had come. He almost expected her to come and check in on him and Zamon personally wanting to see with her own eyes how they both were doing.

"What's up, Mama Cora?" He replied.

"My child, just call me Cora. You make me feel old when you speak to me like that." She offered him a smile.

He gave her a weak smile right back.

"I heard about your brother's condition and told one of my little one's to take me to him right now. And I figured that's where I would find you as well." Said Cora as she moved over to stand next to Kaedon. She wrapped an arm around his waist and laid her head upon his shoulder as they both stood there looking at Zamon.

"They say he might not walk again."

"But that's not what the Lord says, my dear. I've witnessed what man says impossible becomes a possibility. So, keep hope alive and never lose faith in the Lord."

"I will," he nodded.

That's when the old lady turned fully to face him and gazed up into Kaedon's eyes. She held his gaze for a very long time before she finally spoke up again. "What you did this morning, it took courage and a great man to do. I admire you, Kaedon."

"What're you talkin' about, Cora?"

"I'm talking about you proposing to my granddaughter with a promise to love, honor, and cherish her forever. No man would make a vow like that, Kaedon. You are something truly special and I thank God that he brought someone like you to bring color into our lives," she said.

He didn't reply.

Cora continued. "If I didn't know better, I'd believe that God is testing you with all this mess."

"I don't know what for," he finally replied. "I don't like being tested."

"Then get out there and do what needs to be done, Kaedon. The Lord doesn't make mistakes," she said and got a surprised reaction from him. "He doesn't, my child. So why are you standing in here feeling sorry for yourself for not being more protective over your family when you could be out there utilizing that time earning them back. I don't condone violence, but I wasn't always a flower either. But in order to get our family back and bring closure to our lives is to go for what you know."

"And you know what that is, Cora?" Kaedon doubted very much that she knew what his life was actually like.

"I know exactly what that is, Kaedon."

"What?" He asked her.

Cora put her fists on her lips and sucked her teeth with attitude. "Stop trying to be cute, love. You have 'gangsta' written all over you. I'm sure you put that title on the shelf to focus on raising your family. But now it's time to put that lifestyle back to good use to go take back what belongs to you."

"Enough said, Cora. I gotcha," he replied.

"I was done talking anyway," she said and went over to sit down in the chair next to the window. Cora then pulled out her bible from her big black purse and flipped it to the book of Psalms.

One more look at his brother, Kaedon, said a silent prayer for him, then headed for the door. When he opened the door he froze instantly, for the last person he expected to see was standing right there before his eyes.

"Long time no see, Kaedon. Or do you still prefer to be called Murda-K?" Said the unexpected visitor.

Kaedon just couldn't believe his eyes. "Fuck," he replied.

The elemental of surprise.

Chapter 8

When Kaedon saw Aaron "Meatball" Anthony standing before him it took him back to when he last seen his homeboy after he became one of America's Most Wanted. That was fourteen years ago when he and Meatball went on a murder mission together to knock off the witnesses who threatened to stand trial on Twan for robbing that jewelry store. A week after that Meatball was said to have killed a police officer during a traffic stop in Tallahassee on Christmas Eve. That was a tragedy so long ago. Meatball had been missing in action ever since and yet here he was standing in front of Kaedon. The nigga looked different with age, but Kaedon could never miss the big ears and big soup cooler lips that was Meatball's endless childhood butt of jokes. About four years older than Kaedon, Meatball still sustained his youthful look minus the big palm-tree dreadlocks.

"I thought you was dead, my nigga." Kaedon gave him a brief hug.

"I am." Meatball smirked.

"Understood. Damn, my nigga. I can't believe you're here right now, Meatball." Kaedon was genuinely happy to see him.

"It's not Meatball no more, brah. It's Amod now."

Kaedon nodded his understanding. "Cool."

After looking around them in obvious caution, Meatball, AKA Amod, told Kaedon he didn't feel comfortable out in the open like that.

So, Kaedon beckoned him to follow as they headed for the exit route of the big hospital. Kaedon was so anxious to know all about Amod's new life and what it's been like for the past fourteen years on the run. Everybody from their hometown has written him off as dead.

For ten years Amod had been bouncing around throughout the whole United States and staying below the radar. He'd taken his show on the road putting his pistol game down and bodying niggas on every corner. It was his way to eat and survive in the game. Amod went from being a real hitter to being an Uber driver to jacking dope boys and even working a construction job in New Jersey just to have something honest to do. But that was before he met a beautiful woman from the Virgin Islands named Krystal Marie and fell in love and changed up his whole game plan after resting there in New Orleans.

At hearing this Kaedon halted and turned his gaze on the man who had been a true player to the women coming from where they came from. "You? A family man? How?" He said.

"Love, my nigga. Delani and Demani, both about to be six years old come November."

"Wait a minute. Are you talkin' about twins?"

"Yeah. Why?"

Kaedon felt his heart lurch with excitement. "That's crazy, my nigga. That hospital room you just saw me leave out of? That was the room my identical twin brotha is in, brah. Real shit. This is all so crazy to me right now, Amod."

"So, you got a twin brotha?"

Kaedon nodded.

"Bullshit. How the fuck?" And gave Kaedon a look of disbelief, because the only brother he knew of was Twan. They had killed three people for Twan. he was more a brother than a friend. First Kaedon pulled out his cell phone and showed him the proof in black and white. In the process he told Amod how he came about learning about Zamon and what brought them to New Orleans in the first place. When Amod heard this and seeing the truth in Kaedon's eyes, he laid a hand upon his shoulder and told him that it was destined that they reunited.

"In the last four years since I've been living here, my nigga, I've been keepin' tabs on what's going on in the streets."

"I can't ask you to get involved in all this shit, Meatball," said Kaedon with a humbled expression. He already knew where he was going by the statement he made.

"You're not asking me shit because I'm insisting, nigga. And besides, I can't watch you go through nothing and not get involved." A long silence passed between them.

"You got your tool with you?"

"Nah. I took the plane here," said Kaedon. "But I need me one."

"Just chill, my nigga. You're in good hands. I got everything you need back at the house."

Kaedon didn't know whether to feel good about Amod getting involved, because after what has happened to the others already only made him weary. But with Amod on his side they could do some serious damage. Then all it took was for Kaedon to think back on their last mission together. It gave him that inspiration that he needed to change his heart back to cold blackness. There was blood in his eyes now.

The streets of New Orleans better get ready because there was a new gangsta in town.

***

Sometime near midnight Beno pulled up outside the westside home residence of his sister's and honked the horn twice. Romell stepped outside the front door of the house dressed in all black. He looked both ways up the streets surveying his surroundings. Clutching his gun to his side and looking out towards the car at the curb, Romell noticed that it wasn't one he recognized. Tonight, Beno was rolling in a classic Pontiac Grand Prix. After a moment of deciding, Romell made his way to the car and got in.

"Thought you was gonna just stand there all night," Beno said to him with a blunt in his hand.

"Gotta scope out the scenery. It's a jungle out here. A nigga can't be too careful."

"You're right about that, brah."

"Let's get to it and tell me what you know." Romell gestured for the road ahead and Beno sent the car moving forward.

As they rode through the night Beno filled him in on what he had learned so far. Through some of the details Romell had already gotten from the local news channel that evening that he had killed three people and injured two others. Neither one of them was Lance, but he had slumped his little protege Benji in the process. When Romell looked at Benji's photo plastered on the TV that evening it gave him a hard-on. He was excited knowing that Trenika was suffering from the deaths. The primary target was Lance but everybody who fell around him was enough to deem a successful mission.

Beno went on to say that no one knew where Trenika was, that she had run away with her daughter. When Romell heard this his whole world stopped turning. A daughter? He hadn't known she had a little girl. How old was this daughter? Where had she been when he was shooting up the place?

Something about that revelation didn't sit well with Romell and he needed more intel on that situation.

A daughter? He wondered with a devilish smirk.

How Romell had learned of Trenika's whereabouts down in Quincy, Florida was through her paintings. Romell had always told her that she would become famous one day. So, after believing that she wouldn't get a normal job using her real name and needed something to keep up a steady income, Trenika would depend on her art to provide for her. All it took was for him to look into the art world and search some of the galleries promoting independent artists. After about two years of searching and paying close attention to the painting's details and its signed trademark signature, Romell struck gold and began digging deeper into where the paintings originated from. Advanced technology was a god sent to the world of electronic devices because it didn't take him long after discovery to pinpoint Trenika's location.

All of this Romell had done while in prison with a simple smartphone smuggled in through Layla. His real ride or die bitch that literally worshiped the ground he walked on.

"I know you heard about the hit on Boss Hog," Beno replied as they cruised through the city streets bumping some Mo3 and vibing on some real shit.

Romell heard all about the shooting at the local diner where Boss Hog was said to be meeting with another major drug lord by the name of Levy Mustafa, who is from Benin City in the Edo State of Nigeria. The whole alphabet unit was all over that case for sure and Romell wanted no parts in that. Word on the streets was that the Nigerian was Boss Hog's new connect, and with his death would surely bring in loads of trouble for the city.

"It's better him than me," said Romell, wondering if Lance even gave a fuck or not. Because if anything his whole family could get wiped off the face of this earth if his involvement was to get to the wrong people.

"The streets is on fire out there right now, brah. Niggaz are closing shops down and going underground for the time being. Especially those who were against Boss Hog's going into power with the new connect and all," said Beno.

"Maybe we can whisper Lance's name in there somewhere," Romell suggested with a head nod.

"Then that would beg the question of how I know, which could lead back to you and they wipe us all down just because we were in the know."

"You got a valid point, Beno." Romell thought of the way with how fast Beno shifted the matter away from him. Because Romell damn sure was going to have him do it himself.

But then there was that unshakable reminder that Trenika had a daughter which made him very uneasy.

"I need you to find out more on that little girl that Trenika has," he said. Romell didn't want to entertain the current thoughts he was having concerning the little girl. He would keep that to himself until he learned more on the situation. Because if this little girl was between five or six then there was a serious problem that he had on his hands. "I need to know this by tomorrow," he stressed.

Chapter 9

The following morning Trenika woke up to the news of the vicious murders that transpired the day before. For some reason she felt as though all the killings that took place within the last 24 hours had been initially related to her situation.

From back down in Atlanta with the murder of Nikolai to the dozen or so murders there in New Orleans had her dizzy with worry about what was going to happen next.

Trenika sent Kaedon and Lance and Jhene and all the rest of her friends and family a healthy text message to reassure them all that she was okay. Last night Cindy had purchased her a new phone after stepping out for some Chinese takeout. It was a burner phone that wouldn't lead back to them. The lawyer was indeed a sweet but swift individual when she wanted to be. And Trenika could only imagine how swift and dedicated she was in the courtroom.

While Aryanna still slept after purposefully keeping her up all night for just that reason. Trenika entered the home office to boot up the laptop computer. She wanted to check social media traffic to see what all she could learn about what was going on around her. People had a habit of posting all of the right and wrong shit on social media.

And sure enough, she got all the juicy details on what was going on. Someone even had the audacity to record the shooting incident that transpired inside the diner yesterday morning. While people were getting killed this idiot was standing nearby recording the shit like it was some scene out of a horror movie. It was dumb shit like that that gets people killed.

Trenika shook her head sadly as she finished reviewing the inside scoop on what's going on in the streets. But there were four posts on Facebook that she read by Jhene, Pooh Baby, Davida and Lance's girlfriend Quanda, messaging how much they loved her and were praying for her and Aryanna's safety, and that they were all working on bringing her back to them. While reading this Trenika cried softly because she knew how scared everybody was for them. They also knew she would eventually seek out their Facebook pages and get the message. But one message really stood out to her and that was the one by Quanda, whom she knew without a doubt was her brother's doing.

"Oh Lance," Trenika stared at the animated picture of a handgun with smoke swirling up out of its barrel. It was an indication that he was out there taking care of business or would avenge the deaths of their loved ones.

"You know that is just as dangerous as leading a person straight to your front door," Cindy said from the doorway.

"I know. Social media is a death trap, I've witnessed what it could do. But it's news, it's informational, and I need to know what the streets is saying so I'll know what my next move would be." Said Trenika as she turned around to face the other woman. From the looks of it Cindy had just taken a shower because her hair still appeared damp and her milky skin was clammy with shower water.

"Well, just be careful, honey. I gotta get to work." Cindy replied. "Got a busy day ahead of me."

Trenika nodded.

After Cindy left the house for work thirty minutes later, Aryanna got up and was given breakfast. While she ate Trenika was snatched out of her concentration by the ring of the doorbell. This left Trenika wary because Cindy assured her that she didn't take visits often, unless it was by family and the few close friends she did have, and that they all knew she spends most of her time at the firm and in court during the day. So, whoever was at the front door apparently knew Cindy was gone to work and that left Trenika suspicious.

When she finally made it to the front door and peered into the peephole, Trenika almost let out a scream. Then she hurriedly unlocked the door and opened it immediately.

"I found you."

"Kaedon." Her eyes welled up with tears. "I'm sorry."

"Daddy!" came Aryanna's voice as she squealed with glee behind Trenika and rushed by her into Kaedon's arms. "I knew you would come! I dreamed it! I love you, daddy," Aryanna said as she hugged his neck and rested her head upon his shoulder, squeezing him tightly.

"I love you, too," he said. Kaedon stared into Trenika's eyes and stepped forward to enter the house.

Behind him stood another man that Trenika didn't recognize but nodded in his direction respectively. She knew that if he was with her man then he could be trusted.

"I'm curious, Kaedon. How did you know?" Asked Trenika as he followed her family into the living room.

"Of all the people you chose to keep you safe, it had to be one of the top defense lawyers in the game. It wasn't hard to narrow it down after discovering the surveillance video outside the Wal-Mart you were at and hopped in the truck of Cindy Adams." Kaedon sat down with baby girl in his lap upon the couch.

"I kept tellin' mommy you'd come for us," Aryanna cried as she clung to him.

"You did, baby girl?" He looked at her.

Aryanna nodded anxiously. "You're our hero, daddy."

"Always will be." He kissed her cheek and looked up at his future wife. "Always," Kaedon repeated.

Without saying a word, Trenika sat next to her man and gathered him and her daughter into her arms and cried in total happiness. This was everything she had ever wanted and dreamed of, which was family and security. But she was still scared, very scared indeed.

A monster was out there doing everything it took to take it all away from her.

***

Sometime around 11:00 A.M. that very same morning while at Zamon's bedside, Grandma Cora was in the middle of talking to her daughter Wanda when the door to the room opened and a total of eight people entered.

Cora stood up as she watched the leader, who was a beautiful female that appeared strangely familiar, approached the foot of Zamon's bed and stared down at him quietly.

"Excuse me but who are you, lovely?"

The female looked at the old lady and said, "I'm Tazzy." Zamon and Kaedon are my brothers."

"From California?"

"Yes ma'am," came a sparkling response.

"You've come a very long way for a heartbreak, my dear," said Cora with conviction.

Tazzy shrugged. "I left my heart back home in Cali years ago," she said. "I'm only here for one thang."

"And what's that?" Wanda asked.

"Vengeance for what was done to my brother." Tazzy shot a cold glance in the other woman's direction. The instant she learned about the killing yesterday afternoon, she rounded up her team of Crips and financed the flight straight over to New Orleans on one of her associate's private jet, to come put that murder game down.

Her intentions were clear to both older women by the looks of the seven grim faced killaz standing behind her. There was no doubt that under her slightest whim they would kill without a question as to why they were doing it.

Tazzy was very influential and a powerful bitch.

57

She was dangerous.

"Have you spoken with Kaedon yet?" Cora asked.

"I texted him on the way here to the hospital," Tazzy answered moments before the door opened suddenly and Kaedon entered the room carrying baby girl with Trenika and AMod taking up the back. Upon seeing her brother again a wicked smirk appeared on Tazzy's face.

For the next minute or so they all watched the interchange of Trenika and the two older women reuniting after taking such great losses as they did. Cora took control of the situation and made the appropriate introductions.

One look at Tazzy and her crew was all Trenika needed to see to know what they were there for.

Next, Kaedon excused himself and his now bigger team of killaz and exited the room. Tazzy ordered two of her men to stand guard outside Zamon's room door while her and Kaedon led the rest of them back outside.

"Flame, Tony. Y'all go get the cars ready to head out. I'll roll with Kaedon and his man," Tazzy replied and her two men hurried to go retrieve their vehicles.

Meanwhile, Amod went to retrieve his car just as Lance, Boogie, and two more of their men pulled up on the scene in a big Audi Q8 SUV strapped with heavy artillery.

Enroute to the hospital Kaedon had phoned Lance to inform him that he'd found Trenika and baby girl. Lance had already been in the streets lurking with his own crew.

"Where y'all headed?" Lance asked them.

"To my partna Amod's spot over—" Kaedon was cut off.

"I already know, brah. I know Amod. I fucks with that nigga. Just let me go in and see Iss and the fam, and I'll meet y'all there?" Said Lance, climbing out of the big SUV equipped with a bullet proof vest strapped on beneath his jacket. Then he ran into the hospital building and disappeared from sight.

"Who was that?" Tazzy asked her brother.

Kaedon looked over at her. "That's my girl's brotha. Lance." He said.

"He's cute," she replied. "He looks official.'

"And solid like a muthafucker. I respect that young nigga." Kaedon told her. "I trust him." He said.

Minutes later they all piled up into their vehicles and got into traffic. After coming together as one unit, from there the streets of New Orleans would have reason to worry.

It was about to go down.

Chapter 10

Once again, social media has been the link to some very crucial information that led to some very profound truth. And that truth lied on the Instagram of Davida's in the photo of a little beautiful girl named Aryanna. The same Aryanna that shared the same nose, wide forehead, and the same sharp chin and big brown eyes as him. The beautiful child was the splitting image of him, and Romell felt like he was about to faint.

Romell did the mental mathematics of the last time him and Trenika had sex prior to her running away. The estimation outcome matched the age that Aryanna was. She was five years old and biologically his child. There was no question who she was. Aryanna was his daughter for sure.

This angered Romell to the core. He hadn't known Trenika was pregnant with his child.

Yesterday when he pulled that stunt of his, one of those bullets could have hit his daughter. Just the thought of that happening made him shudder with discontent. Had Trenika told Aryanna about him. Does she know that that other guy wasn't her father? Who was he anyhow? Romell had to switch his game up now that Aryanna was relevant. He wondered if taking Aryanna for himself would really make Trenika suffer. If that's the case then he had to penetrate the wall of protection she had revolving around her.

Romell would direct his focus on Aryanna now, since Trenika wanted to be cruel and keep her away from him.

He wanted his daughter.

He wanted to make his baby mama go crazy.

As he rode through the city in a dark haze of sinister intention, Romell smiled at the thought of what he planned to do about Trenika and her so-called revenge against him by keeping his daughter away from him. Romell drove over to the meeting place him and Beno agreed to at the Four Seasons hotel across town. He said he had some vital information for him.

Upon reaching the hotel Romell parked his car out front two spaces over from Beno's vehicle. He sent his baby mama's brother a text and after waiting a few minutes Beno was sliding into the passenger seat of the car.

"Talk to me, brah. What's the word?" Romell said while freaking his fresh Black & Mild cigar to smoke.

"The word is ticket, Romell," Beno began as he fired up a Newport cigarette. "You have a fifty-thousand-dollar ticket on your head, dead or alive. Niggaz is really out there loking for you, my nigga. It's bad. That nigga Lance is financing the hit and he's teaming up with muthafuckerz. Word on the streets right now is Lance got niggaz from way out in Cali and other muthafuckin' places d'ing up to get you. I'm tellin' you, brah, you need to stay low," Beno said with a long pull from his cigarette.

"Is that right?" Romell muttered as he stared straight forward in deep thought and fired up his cigar.

"Another thing too before I forget," said Beno.

"What?"

Beno said, "The dude who was proposing to your girl name is Kaedon Smith. His twin brother's name is Zamon Newman. Zamon is the one over at the hospital right now shot the fuck up. But he got two tough-lookin' niggaz standing guard outside his room door."

"Where are you gettin' this information, Beno?"

"I got this lil' snowbunny bitch I'm fuckin' that works as a nurse at the hospital," he said.

"What's her name?"

Reluctantly, Beno looked over at him and immediately sensed something troubling before answering Romell's question. "Amber Trischler," he replied uneasily in the passenger seat.

With a nod, Romell thought about Beno and whether he was loyal enough not to earn that $50,000 for his head. Could he be trusted to keep his mouth shut? Because if killing Beno right now that could direct attention to Layla, which would eventually lead to his whereabouts.

Without further ado, Romell started the car and backed out of the parking space. When Beno asked him where they were going he told Beno to sit back and relax, that he had something to show him before they made their next move. But what Romell was about to do was take the life of his baby mama's brother and bury him where Beno won't be discovered. After he told Romell about the money on his head, he wasn't going to risk it and give Beno the opportunity to even consider it.

Like Romell once said, he played for keeps.

The stakes were too high now to take chances like that so he will put an end to that possibility. Layla will have to deal with a broken heart when her brother ends up missing. All that time Romell spent behind the wall plotting and scheming, he'd be damned if he allowed a nigga like Beno to stop him from accomplishing his mission.

No one is to be spared from his vengeance.

Not even Layla was exempt from his wrath when he got to the point of feeling his back was against the wall.

***

Everybody had settled in Amod's spot, which was a warehouse unit where he conducted his business hooking up custom made paint jobs and cars' sound systems, and detailing. It was big enough inside to shelter three eighteen-wheeler trucks. And Amod even provided refreshments as they all gathered around and discussed the seriousness of their current situation.

Tazzy was impressed with the actions Kaedon had taken the night before. He and Amod had caught a few of Benji's enemies slipping and slaughtered them mercilessly. Amod knew what was going on in the streets and had filled Kaeden in on what was going on too. So, Kadon wanted to honor Benji' death by going after his enemies. After taking a few lives in cold blood it awakened that beast in him that's been dying to be set free.

Lance arrived twenty minutes later. Him, Boogie, and the two others who he introduced as Wanky and Ralo, entered the warehouse like a pack of wolves. They sized up the blue bandana wearing gangstaz, and Lance made it clear that he wasn't comfortable with their presence. Explaining that their presence could present the wrong impression to the widespread of Bloods that polluted the surrounding areas.

"We are who we are, cuz." Said Tazzy. "But I also am in business with a few top Blood members back out west that'll contact your people down here." The rest didn't need to be explained what was understood.

Lance looked over to Boogie, who was also a Blood member along with one of the other two men. Boogie spoke up and demanded that he needed the contact information out west so he could justify their current situation.

"No problem," Tazzy acknowledged one of her men by the name of Slow-Loc and told him to handle the situation.

Both Boogie and Slow-Loc broke off from the rest of them and stepped aside to conduct business. Gang banging wasn't the same as how it used to be back in the days where wearing the wrong thing could get you killed without question. Where a bloody war transpired between two gangs solely because one was caught in the wrong area. Nowadays the two most notorious gangs in the U.S. are learning to unify when necessary and exercise the act of growth and development.

Meanwhile, Lance approached Kaedon with the most amazing news he'd heard since Romell invading his world became a hindrance.

"I got an address," said Lance.

"Is it accurate though?" Asked Kaedon. He didn't want to make the mistake of killing the wrong people who had nothing to do with Romell. He wanted Romell and everybody he loved.

"I remembered you telling me about the lawyer chick that sis had been laying low with. I thought if one person could get that type of info on Romell it would be a lawyer. So, I got my lawyer guy to pull some strings for me and this is what I was given in the process," Lance then produced a printed copy of Romell's release form from the pocket of his Levis.

Kaedon held the unfolded paper and scanned the information printed upon the paper. "Layla Miller," he whispered the name as Amod came to stand beside him.

"Twenty-two fifty-seven Fielding Lane." Amod read the printed address on the paper.

Right at that moment Wanky stepped forward and said that he was familiar with the street of the address. "I have a lil' bitch that lives out there. Who did you say lives there?" He asked.

"Some chick name Layla," said Kaedon

Wanky perked up at the name. "Damn, Lance, why didn't you tell me this shit beforehand?" He looked over at his homeboy. "That's that nigga Beno's sista." He said.

"Beno," Lance repeated the name.

"Who's this nigga Beno?" Kaedon wanted to know what he was up against.

A real bitch ass nigga who thinks his hustle game could solve all his problems. He's no real threat. The nigga got a habit with paying niggaz to get their hands dirty for him. Beno's a dead man now," said Lance with conviction.

Wanky had his share of words on Beno too. It was obvious no one thought highly of Beno and that alone was all the reason for Kaedon to believe Romell would associate himself with such a character.

"Okay," Kaedon turned to Wanky and said, "Think you can get your chick to go over and play nice with Layla just to peep out the scenery and get back with you?"

"I can do it," he answered.

"Make that call," Kaedon ordered. In the process, he wanted to go get the lay of the land as well. "And I want somebody to find Beno and... Bring him here? We need all the information he got on Romell." He was looking at Amod and Amod gave him an agreeing head nod.

It was crunch time.

Today Romell will die a hard death.

Chapter 11

Speaking of which, Romell turned the car into the entrance of an old dirty wooden house driveway that circled around to the back. He parked the car, and Beno turned a questioning glance over at him.

They had driven all the way to Baton Rouge to get to this location. Romell told him that he had ran down on a nigga Beno knew as Swizz Mcintosh, who was indeed an archenemy of his. It was said that Swizz had sent some goons to rob Beno for some work a couple of weeks ago. Of course, Beno had his suspicions but he didn't think Swizz would pull a move like that. He wasn't the jack boy type of niggas, but to hear differently now made Beno believe an enemy was capable of anything.

But why not kill him when the jack move could have ended with his life without anyone being the wiser? Thought Beno as his adrenaline began to rush through him.

Romell said this mission would prove his loyalty to him and bond them by blood.

"Is Swizz really in there?" Asked Beno

"Down in the basement," said Romell after opening the door and getting out of the car.

Hesitantly, Beno did the same while patting the Ruger P90 pistol that he had tucked at his waist. Ever since the scare of him being robbed and assaulted recently, arming himself with his own tool was a necessity. Not saying that he wasn't always strapped, the incident only made him more cautious to begin packing two pistols. The PPK .380 pistol in his ankle holster was the unexpected, but also necessary weapon that many would not expect him to have.

Beno was far from a dumb nigga.

He watched as Romell used what looked like an old butter knife he'd picked up off the back porch to use to jimmy the lock on the backdoor. Once opened Romell tossed the butter knife aside and pushed the door open and entered the old abandoned house.

Scanning the area surrounding the back of the house for anything worth being cautious of, he didn't find any and climbed onto the back porch for the door.

"Whew!" Beno covered a hand over his nose when he stepped through the backdoor of the house. "Smells like a muthafucker is dead in this bitch already," he said.

"Shut the door, brah." Romell replied.

Beno did as he was told and kicked the back door shut behind him.

Thinking back on his knowledge of things, Beno knew this was the same house that once belonged to Romell's aunt Debbie. The very same house that Lance and Benji killed Debbie, her ten-year-old son, and sister Kimberly. Was it their deaths that still permeated throughout the house as Beno followed his sisters' baby daddy up the dark hallway? He wondered as he moved with calculated steps.

A minute later Romell paused at the basement door and glanced back at Beno.

"What's up?" Beno came to a halt in front of him.

Romell smirked devilishly over at him.

Just when Beno was about to say something he felt a thick arm snake around his neck from behind and applied tremendous pressure. Beno panicked and reached for the pistol at his waist. But Romell beat him to it and snatched the weapon away from him and placed the gun to his forehead.

"It's time you pay the piper, brah."

"Noo!" Beno struggled against the chokehold that cut off all air supply as dizziness overtook him.

"Lights out, muthafucker!" Snarled Romell.

Beno let out another fearful cry as darkness fell over him and slumped in the arms of his unknown attacker. But Romell was very aware who he was, whom many people had counted out since his incarceration ten years ago. Which was his cousin Manny, whose brother Oscar was killed during Lance's blood thirst on that fateful night years ago.

Having been released from prison four months prior to Romell, Manny was the quiet storm that Romell also had manipulated the control over since they were reunited behind the wall together. There would always be one and Romell was going to use his cousin for all it was worth until they both had sought vengeance finally.

Romell knew exactly what he was doing, and Manny would be the tool to make sure he emerged victoriously.

Or so he thought...

***

Trenika couldn't stop thinking about what her brother had told her concerning Romell. Her mind had been so unnerved by the knowledge of him being so close to her loved ones all this time. But it's who he had been romantically involved with that really made her furious.

And that's why she called Jhene and told her to stop what she was doing and get there to the hospital. Because once Jhene heard what she had to say there was no question her friend would want to press the issue.

While waiting on her friend to arrive, Trenika turned to her grandmother and looked the older woman in the eyes. Then she told her what was on her mind and what she wanted to do about it.

"Absolutely not!" Cora shook her head as she watched Trenika rise up to her feet. "Trenika," she said and stood up next. "I cannot allow you to do that, it's too dangerous. Besides, Kaedon will take care of everything. There's no need for you to get involved."

"I'm already involved, Ma." She argued.

"I said no," she retorted, glaring at Trenika.

Trenika said, "I love you, but my mind is made up, Mama. I know what I'm doing. Just watch over baby girl," she glanced over at her daughter who was asleep at the foot of Zamon's bed.

Also occupying the room was aunt Wanda, cousin Pearl and Pooh Baby, and Trenika's godmother Tamia, who was her brother Lance's pride and joy. Davida was also there but had left out to go confer with her former colleagues. Everybody watched both Trenika and Cora go back and forward with each other.

When Tamia attempted to intervene, Trenika snapped at her and said, "I'm a grown ass woman, and if I wanna go out there and handle my business how I wanna, then I will."

"Trenika…" Grandma Cora replied evenly.

"It's done," said Trenika as she headed for the door and let herself out. Outside in the hallway she motioned for one of Tazzy's men to follow her. With a silent nod from his partner the Crip gangsta followed Trenika up the hall towards the exit of the building.

When it was just the two of them in the elevator, she asked him what his name was.

"Midnight," he answered.

"Okay, Midnight," Trenika looked at him with interest and saw that he was indeed blacker than Wesley Snipes and saw why he had such a name. "Do you have an extra piece on you I can have?"

"A gun?" He looked at her with skepticism.

"Yeah. Don't look like that. I'm licensed to carry. I just don't feel comfortable without one."

"That's what I'm here for, Trenika."

"I don't know you, cuz. All I'm asking is to be—" Trenika ceased her words when Midnight reached behind him and handed her a Glock .23 pistol.

"What you know about that there?" He smirked.

Without a word Trenika dropped the clip with one hand, snatched it out the air with the other hand to check the magazine, and slapped it back in with a brief nod. "It'll get the job done," she said.

Midnight almost thought he was in love but knew he would just have to settle for respect.

Minutes later they met Jhene at the front lobby of the hospital where Trenika took her by the hand and guided her back out through the door. Jhene had declared a family emergency to her boss at the local insurance agency and took off without a backward glance.

Back behind the wheel of her car, Jhene listened without interruption as Trenika dropped the bomb on her. As she heard her friend out Jhene felt herself become angered by what was being said.

Midnight sat in the back quiet as kept but watching the area around them in the busy hospital parking lot. He had his twin Glock .23 resting in his lap.

The situation was, Layla Miller used to be their friend before she moved over to the westside and got brand new on them. Then Layla ended up siding with her cousin Brandy who had testified against Angie's uncle Clive that sent him to prison for twenty-five years for a home invasion charge. That was about ten years ago and since then, Jhene and Angie had fought with Layla, and Trenika beat Brandy to sleep right in her front yard. Now here it was years later Layla was involved with Romell, and probably was the help he needed to locate her.

"Small world," Midnight replied. "That's wild, cuz."

Trenika nodded grimly. "And very cold too," she said with coldness in her tone. "That bitch is about to get what she shoulda been got years ago."

This time when Jhene looked at her friend, she would have sworn that she saw a murderous glare in her eyes.

Scared now, Jhene finally let it register just what Trenika's intentions were at that moment.

To kill Layla.

Chapter 12

Kaedon and his crew rode past Layla's house and didn't spot no vehicle in the driveway. Two minutes behind them Lance and his crew did the same thing.

That's when Kaedon got the call from his girl's brother and picked up on the first ring. Amod was at the wheel of the car and Tazzy was in the back with one of her men. The artillery her and her team had brought along with them was something out of a Brad Thor novel. Kaedon was almost afraid to be in the same vehicle with the type of weapons they had.

"I'm listening," he said into the phone anxiously.

"It's Wanky," came the response and Kaedon absentmindedly peered into the rearview mirror as though he could see the other man in the Audi truck behind them.

"What's up, Wanky? I don't trust these phones."

"Me neither, dawg," said Wanky. "But I just spoke with my chick and she said no one was home. That one of the cars normally parks out back behind the crib and it wasn't there. But she did mention the bitch was probably at work today."

"Where does she work?" Kaedon asked.

"At the new indoor flea market they got downtown."

Kaedon glazed over at Amod and asked him did he know where that was and he said he did. Before hanging up with Wanky, he also learned about Romell's significant other having a four-year-old kid too. At hearing this, Kaedon put the phone down and allowed his current thoughts to take over.

He shared this information with his crew and Tazzy wanted to handle the situation with Layla. She wanted to use her finesse game to lure Layla out into their trap. Tazzy was good at doing such things and assured Kaedon that Layla would trust another feminine face than one of a cold-hearted on such as the likes of him.

"I'ma let you do you, sis," said Kaedon

"All you want is Romell," Tazzy stated matter-of-factly.

"Correct," he confirmed.

They headed back in town while Tazzy gave them the strategy in which she planned to use to lure Layla out. She already knew what she looked like from her Facebook and Instagram account. Layla was a beautiful woman, very sexy, but Tazzy knew a weak bitch when she saw one.

Kaedon wanted to also do something he knew Romell would never expect. "After we grab Layla, we're gonna take her home to her house." He stated.

"I already know where you're going with this," said Amod.

"Me too," said Po'Boi in the back seat next to Tazzy who was her appointed right hand man.

"Just get me to this bitch Layla." Tazzy interjected. She couldn't even stay still; she was so anxious to do some gangsta shit to quench her thirst for blood.

About halfway there Kaedon received a call from Davida and wondered what she wanted. Upon seeing her number, it brought thoughts of Zamon to mind and he hurriedly answered the phone, with hopes that everything was alright.

"You're not gonna believe this shit, Kaedon." Davida sounded more upset than worried.

"What's there not to believe?"

"That that silly woman of yours had gone after Romell's woman and there's no tellin' what she is about to do."

"What!" Kaedon's heart dropped.

"She took one of them Crip boys with her too."

"What!" This really had Kaedon on edge as he listened to Davida fill him in on the confrontation Trenika had with their grandmother before rushing out. Kaedon looked over at Amod and told him what he just learned, stressing that they needed to get to Layla before Trenika did.

"Damn, brah," said Tazzy. "You got yourself a gangsta bitch already, you don't need my help."

"Shut the fuck up, Tazzy!" He sneered back at her and she held her hands up. "Right now isn't the time, sis."

"It's time for murder." She added.

Minutes later they appeared just in time to see Trenika forcing Layla into the trunk of her own car at gunpoint. Also with her was Tazzy's man, Midnight, who glared up at them while keeping his hand close to the gun tucked at his waistline. When Amod pulled up on the scene both Kaedon and Tazzy got out of the car at once.

"What the fuck you think you're doing, Trenika?" Kaedon rushed her the moment she shut the trunk closed with Layla inside. He then took the gun from her and shoved her roughly back towards the car. "You must be outta your fuckin' mind."

"I got this under control, Kae."

"You've done enough, baby. Get in the car." Kaedon ordered her and glared when she hesitated.

"This ain't the time or place for drama, sis." Tazzy looked at her and said in that serious tone of hers.

Reluctantly, Trenika snatched the gun back from Kaedon and got into the car behind Amod. Next Tazzy retrieved the car keys from Midnight and slid behind the wheel of Layla's car. It was then that Po'Boi and Midnight jumped into the car, with her and Kaedon back in the front seat next to Amod. one after the other they all peeled out and got into traffic with Jhene's car at the rear.

"You've got some fuckin' nerve, Trenika." Kaedon said once they were away from the scene. If Davida wouldn't have put him up on game and Amod not flooring the car all the way there, they would have missed Trenika. And that alone sent a cold chill running up Kaedon's spine.

Trenika muttered something under her breath.

"What did you just say?" Kaedon said, turning around in his seat to face her.

"I said 'You're not the only one who can do some gangster shit.' Kaedon Smith." She rolled her eyes and folded her arms over her chest in that stubborn way of hers.

With the shake of his head, Kaedon didn't know whether to laugh or cry. In his heart of hearts he loved Trenika more after witnessing what she did moments ago. He knew she had that spark in her, but never in a million years would he have imagined her doing that.

That really was some gangsta shit, he noted.

Trenika's gangsta couldn't be denied even if he wanted to. Today she proved just how thorough she was and Kaedon had to give respect when her respect is due.

***

Killing Beno was very necessary because he couldn't be as trustworthy as Romell wished he had been. With that type of money on his head, Romell doubted the nigga would have kept it solid with him. Money ruled niggas like Beno, he would have eventually sold him out.

After killing Beno, he was buried in the ground beneath the basement floor of the house. Prior to bringing him there Manny had already dug the grave in the floor. The nigga had literally dug it six feet deep, which must have been a very strenuous task. Digging graves for human bodies one had to be dedicated and strong. And even filling the grave back up with the dirt it came from was a chore of its own as well.

But Romell and Manny got it done in good timing, where they worked together to accomplish the task. Just like when they took turns torturing information out of Beno before killing him. He went as far as giving up the code to his floor safe at his home, and even the time, dates, and location of the drop off shipments of drugs belonging to one of the biggest dope boys in the city. Beno gave information that wasn't even demanded of him, he just wanted the torture to cease.

Back outside in the bright sunshine, Romell made his way back to the car and got in. His next move was to go deal with Beno's snowbunny chick that he claimed knew way too much.

"I gotta drop by the house first and get myself right before we take it to her," said Romell to his cousin as Manny climbed into the passenger seat.

"I wanna look into that other shit that Beno was babbling about," said Manny.

"The safe or the shipment dropoff?"

"All that shit, cuz."

"If what he said is true about the shipment, nine times out of ten we'll be outnumbered. I know all about Ron Jones and 'em, that's that nigga Juvie's people, and them nigga's roll deep. To hit a spot like that we'll have to do some recruiting first." Romell said. He knew how his cousin felt about such opportunities as that, for it would definitely put him back on his feet. Back in the day Manny was doing big things in the drug trade himself, but he made the mistake of using his own supply and that led to his fall from grace.

Manny sighed audibly, "sure would be nice though. Until then we'll just hit up that safe, my nigga. My pockets is tight right now." he said.

"I gotcha, cuz. Real shit. Just lemme stop by the crib right quick." Romell told him.

In the process, Manny was going through Beno's cell phone and reading his old text messages and checking the call history. He wanted to see what Beno had going on se he would know how to utilize the phone to point Beno's last plan of action elsewhere, to prevent any future investigation on his whereabouts.

A person's cell phone could be a very powerful device if one had used it correctly.

When Romell finally made it to the house he was surprised to find Layla's car parked in the driveway. For a fleeting moment he wondered if his woman was in there with company, but Romell quickly cast that thought aside. However, she should be at work right now and her being home at that moment was cause for suspicion.

"You're definitely ain't coming back out no time soon now with your woman home, cuz." Manny pointed out.

Romell pulled the car around back just like he always did, wondering what Layla was up to in there. "I'll be right out, cuz. Time is of the essence," he said.

"Time is money," Manny quipped.

"That too," grinned Romell, opening the door and getting out of the car.

No sooner than he got out and was approaching the backdoor of the patio did a premonition overwhelmed him. A second later two armed goons wearing blue bandanas over their faces rounded the corner of the house from Romell's left. Two more appeared from his right and drew down on him. A voice called out to him from behind and Romell glanced back at his cousin. A female toting some type of submachine gun stepped over to the passenger door of the car and filled it with bullet holes the size of a child's fist.

But that was the last thing Romell saw before something bashed him in the back of his head knocking him out cold. It was what Romell would experience when he eventually came to. Would he know he'd fucked up? The end had finally come.

Chapter 13

The next time Romell opened his eyes he found himself bound to a chair and staring directly in the cold hard eyes of the last person he expected to see.

"Wanna know how long I've been sitting here watching you, Romell?" Trenika said, sitting in a folded metal chair two feet away from Romell. "Twenty-one minutes. And the whole time never once did I see the person I once loved. All I see is a monster, a woman's worst nightmare."

"So, you never believed I'd actually loved you, Trenika?" said Romell, his voice scratchy.

That's when Trenika drew her gun and sat it on her right thigh, barrel aimed at his stomach with her finger curled around the trigger. "Say the word love one more time and I will kill you dead," she said.

Romell swallowed nervously. The murderous glint in her eyes was all he needed to see to believe that she would kill him without hesitation.

Next Trenika pulled out her cellphone and activated the video icon and turned the face of the phone toward him. "Her name is Aryanna Mahagani, she's five years old, smart, sassy, and very independent. She loves chicken tenders and arts and crafts," smiled Trenika. 'Wanna know what she told me one day? She said when she grows up, she wanted to be the President of the United States so she could have the power to help all the homeless people get off the streets and not suffer. She was four when she told me this. Like I said, she's smart, and one day Aryanna is gonna be a very important woman."

Romell stared at the screen of the phone with tears in his eyes.

On the screen were videos of Aryanna from different stages of her young life. For what seemed like an eternity Romell watched the child that he never got the opportunity to meet. She was everything a father could ever hope for in a daughter, and that made Romell regret his life. Tears spilled silently from his eyes as he knew he would never meet Aryanna, and that he wouldn't have the chance to tell his son goodbye.

When Trenika took the phone away a deep groan of protest escaped him and his chest filled up with burning emotion.

"One thing I want you to do for me if nothing else," Romell said as he looked up at her.

"No. I will not allow Aryanna to get to know her brother. I will no longer have anything to do with you after I take your miserable life."

There was no one else in that warehouse but her and him. Kaedon had heard Trenika out and both him and Lance decided to let her deal with Romell personally. This was the moment that Trenika had always dreamed of. The moment before looking her monster in the eyes before killing him.

"I hope she do become President," he said.

"She will."

Romell smiled. "You ready for this, Tee?"

"Been ready," she said.

"Go ahead. Kill me. Stop bullshittin' and get the job done." He told her. "This is your moment."

Trenika crossed her legs ladylike and aimed the gun at Romell's head. "You die when I'm ready for you to." She said. "Not one damn time did you apologize for giving me H.I.V., Romell. You was ready to die and not even attempt to say how sorry you are for destroying both of our lives. Yes.

Aryanna is affected as well, but she will live to grow a long beautiful, happy life."

Suddenly Romell seemed astounded by her words of expression. He hadn't known she was even affected– his daughter. He was so focused on his own personal grudge that he never considered Aryanna being sick with H.I.V. because of him.

"I'm sorry, Trenika." He said.

"It's too late to apologize." Trenika squeezed the trigger and sent a slug right through Romell's face, snapping his head back violently. She stood up while continually pulling the trigger, sending bullet after bullet into Romell's chest with the intention to burst his cruel heart wide open. All seventeen rounds spent ripping through his flesh was the outcome she sought as her vociferous cries of rage exploded from her with every blast. Even when the blasts from the gun ended, she kept right on bellowing her outrage as she constantly squeezed the trigger. Trenika kept pulling, and with every click, she cursed Romell.

It wasn't until Lance came up behind her and reached out for the gun to lower it. "It's okay," he said stepping in front of her. "You've done it, sis. It's over."

Trenika let her brother take the gun away from her and she threw her arms around him and sobbed against his shoulder. The toughness and all that bravado she had earlier was gone. Trenika was her naturally vulnerable, cordial self again now that her worst nightmare was over.

"Let's take you home." Tazzy appeared and detached the siblings from one another and tossed an arm around her. She gave Lance that silent look that only a gangsta would understand the meaning of, and he nodded.

It was time to clean up the mess.

Romell was dead.

The beginning of a new chapter.

***

Later that night around ten o'clock Kaedon opened the door to Grandma Cora's house and let himself inside. Cora was sitting up front in her rocking chair crocheting something with her needle and yarn the color of red and blue. She looked up at his entry and gave him a straight-faced look. There was no smile, no warmth, the old lady was tired but too stubborn to go to bed.

"Hey, Mama Cee." He greeted her with a kiss on the forehead and a forced smile.

"Is it really over, my dear?" She asked.

"Yes." Kaedon nodded. "It's really over." He said. All evening that's what he, Lance, Tazzy, and Amod were out doing. They were tying up all the loose ends to make sure that come tomorrow, a new journey would begin.

"Okay. I'll take your word for it. Now go to your woman and make sure her heart is whole."

"Thank you, mama," he told her with another kiss.

"Go." Cora said.

Kaedon went straight to Trenika's old childhood bedroom where he knew she was still awake.

Upon entering the bedroom, he found Trenika inside crying softly to herself. Without a word he locked the door and kicked off his sneakers. Then he pulled over his shirt and removed his pants before climbing in bed with his woman that he vowed to love forever.

"Kae…" Trenika whispered his name when he turned her over onto her back and climbed over her.

With the gentlest kiss he silenced her, as his hand stroked her pussy through her panties causing her to moan in much needed pleasure. All she had on was her t-shirt and panties and before he was done with her tonight, she would be totally naked.

Kaedon continued to kiss and stroke her, all the while growing hard and ready to plunge. When his fingers entered her love tunnel Trenika sighed sensually as the breathtaking pleasure he was giving her at that moment was quickening, taking her to that desiring peak.

"I love you so much, Kae." She cried into his lips.

"I love you more." His expert fingers dancing in her were creating a water storm in her panties.

"Don't stop... I need... Please don't stop, Kae." Trenika begged him and he confessed that he didn't plan on stopping. She needed the release that was approaching fast, her body and concierge craving for it.

Kaedon waited and watched her in the darkness, his own body aching to make that connection with her. And when that moment came just before that sweet release, Kaedon pulled her panties aside and entered her deep and raw, causing her to let out a powerful cry of pleasurable rapture. Kaedon covered her mouth with his large hand and continued to drive every inch of himself into her.

After realizing that he had entered her unprotected, Trenika panicked and pushed up against him. But Kaedon only dropped his weight onto her and dug up in her guts like DMX did his girl Keisha in that movie Belly. This was the climatic act of love and devotion towards his woman that Kaedon had grown to accept without regrets.

When Trenika realized she couldn't do anything to stop him, and understanding what this moment meant to Kaedon, she surrendered to him and gave him what he so desired. He gave her the business like never before, pounding her pussy to pieces and making her climax continually. Then when he had finally burst off inside of her, Kaedon kept driving and driving deep into her womb until he was drenched in sweat and had nutted two more times.

Later they laid in one another's arms in the bed and not saying a thing. For a long while they stayed like that until Trenika kissed his shoulder and fell asleep. He held her in his arms all throughout the night.

"No more pain," he muttered softly. "No more fears."

And then sleep claimed him finally. A hero's rest.

Chapter 13

When Trenika woke up the next morning she did so to some unknown force of apprehension of some kind. She sat up in bed and looked over to find Kaedon gone. For a split second she was reminded of the wonderful sex she had the night before by the throbbing sensation between her legs. Then that thought was replaced by that uneasy feeling again.

Trenika scrambled out of bed into a pair of shorts and a t-shirt and headed for the door. The instant she stepped out into the hallway Trenika heard it, it was the unmistakable sound of commotion. She moved in the direction of the noise and found it just outside the back door.

"Don't fret, my child." Grandma Cora said while staring out the back screen door outside. "They're only handling their differences like men." She added.

Trenika stepped past her wide-hipped grandmother and pushed the screen door open to step outside.

Both Kaedon and Josh were shirtless and battling it out with hand-to-hand combat. From the looks of it both men were looking like UFC fighters trading blow for blow and bleeding from busted lips and busted noses. Pound for pound, Kaedon seemed to get the best of Josh, to Trenika's surprise giving the training he'd acquired in the Marines. Josh should be thrashing Kaedon but apparently it was the other way around by the looks of it.

A minute later Kaedon laid Josh out with a dazzling overhand strike that connected with vicious impact.

"Damn," came the response from Lance, who had been leaning against the back of the house the whole time.

Kaedon stepped over Josh and extended his hand out to him. Josh looked up at him and reluctantly took his hand, allowing himself to be pulled up to his feet. Kaedon said something to him that no one could hear. Josh nodded briefly, and then the two men embraced.

"Respect," said Josh

"Respect, my nigga," Kaedon bumped fists with him and turned around to face the people.

Also present out back were Tazzy and her crew, Jhene, and even Josh's best friend Tyler, who also had enlisted for the military and lasted only five years before getting a medical discharge. The differences between Josh and Kaedon were settled and no one favored either man to win. It was a mutual agreement between the two.

Then Trenika descended the porch steps and approached Josh face to face. Kaedon halted for a second but pressed forward and entered the house.

"Where do we stand now, Josh?"

He chucked her across the chin and offered her a bloody but cock grin. "Friends?" He said.

"Always, no matter what." She told him.

"No matter what," he replied. "And Tee…?"

"Yeah?"

Josh said, "You got yourself a good man. I like him to be that one for you."

"He is indeed. I'm happy with Kaedon. And thank you for understanding Josh."

He nodded and she opened out her arms to him, Josh then stepped into her embrace. It was all love and respect.

As he stepped out of her arms. Josh complimented her on her engagement ring and took his leave with Tyler and disappeared around the corner of the house.

Trenika looked down at her left hand and gasped with unexpected astonishment. On her finger was a big diamond ring she didn't notice until just now. Kaedon must have slipped it on while she was asleep. And just gazing at it now was all the evidence she needed to know that Kaedon was in it for the long haul for real.

"It's beautiful," Jhene came over and said. "I so envy you right now, sis."

"It's like a dream come true, Jhene. C'mon, let's go inside, I got so much to tell you." With that being said, the two women hooked their arms together and went inside the house. You couldn't wipe the smile from her face as she glanced down at the rock on her finger and knew there was no turning back.

Trenika was the happiest woman in the world right now.

She was blessed, she honored to be Kaedon's woman, she was her: A gangsta's wife.

***

Tazzy entered the hospital room first with Kaedon stepping inside behind her.

Occupying the room was Zamon's wife and four-month-old son, his brother-in-law Stephen, and his parents, both elder people frowning upon their entry. It was clear that Zamon's parents didn't care too much for Kaedon or Tazzy, whom they blamed for the heartache they both were enduring.

Kaedon greeted everybody humbly, moving over to stand on the side of Zamon's bed. He caught the look of bewilderment that Melody Newman was giving him. The woman, just like all the rest of them, still couldn't believe there were two of them. Although Melody didn't share the same sentiments as her in-laws, she still didn't like the fact that Kaedon had come along and disturbed her life. She understood the importance of getting to know his twin brother but taking him away from his family to which he almost lost his life was too much for her to bear.

When Melody got that phone call she all but lost her mind in the process.

Thanks to Cora, Aunt Wanda, Davida, and all the others who welcomed Melody with open arms, it lessened the resentment she originally had towards Kaedon for not being more protective over his twin brother.

"Man, get up!" Kaedon nudged Zamon awake. "You got everybody in here and all you wanna do is sleep."

Zamon's eyes fluttered open and adjusted his gaze upward to look at his brother. A moment passed before he allowed a weak smile to appear on his face. "Did we win?" He replied hoarsely. "You look like shit."

"Zamon!" His mother protested. "Language," she sighed and turned a glance over at her husband.

"It's over, brah." Kaedon said. "All that's left now is for you to get better and get outta here."

"I can't walk, Kaedon. I'm paralyzed from the waist down. Never in a million years would I have imagined anything like this happening to me. However," Zamon said and coughed a few times before continuing. "My wife always told me that I needed to sit my ass down somewhere," he added.

Melody dropped her head in emotional shame.

"It appears that I'll be sittin' down permanently now," Zamon stated.

"And so you find humor in your situation," said Kaedon.

"I have to or else I'll die miserably."

"Don't say things like that, brother." Tazzy spoke up, reaching down to take Zamon's good hand. "We're gonna make this shit work, cuz. You watch and see. Nothing's changed except for your situation. But you still have your goals and dreams ahead of you to achieve. It just takes some readjusting now, but eventually, Zee, you'll be right back in the groove before you know it."

"I told him the same thing." Melody interjected.

"It's true," Kaedon replied.

After spending the next two hours with Zamon and even accomplishing the task of warming up to his parents, Tazzy and Kaedon took their leave. It was a very sobering experience between the both of them.

"You really think he's gonna pull through, Kaedon?" Asked Tazzy later on that day.

"Of course he will, sis. And when he do we're gonna be right there to goad him on."

"Straight like that, cuz." She responded with a nod.

An awkward silence passed between them.

After waiting on the other to break the silence they turned to look at each other.

"What?" Kaedon was the first to speak up.

"Do you blame yourself for what happened to Zee?" Tazzy had asked the million-dollar question.

Kaedon had heard her loud and clear, but it was an answer that didn't come easily to him. Yet all it took was for her to look into his eyes to see the answer that he could not give verbally. Kaedon blamed himself for what happened to his brother. When Zamon wanted to go back home to his family it was Kaedon that convinced him to visit New Orleans with him. He wanted his twin brother to be there when he made the most important decision of his life by proposing to Trenika.

It was a hard pill to swallow.

He hated himself for it.

Kaedon didn't think he would ever forgive himself. It was a painful reality that he would be reminded of every time he looked in the mirror.

Chapter 14

Five years later.

Trenika and Lisa looked over at each other and laughed as they sat next to each other at The Funny Bone Bar and Lounge. The comedian that was up on stage was a young hilarious black kid who was hustling comics to get by in college. The Funny Bone Bar & Lounge was one of the several business successes that Kaedon was proud of. The place had comedians coming from all over to spit their jewels.

Happily married and blessed with a loving husband and two beautiful children, Trenika had no complaints. Although the past five years weren't a walk in the park, she still made the best of her situation. Trenika couldn't be any happier than the way her life turned out. Her attitude was the sky's the limit and through an unshakable faith, she made a believer out of everybody who ever doubted her.

The owner of her own art gallery and teaching her own art workshop, Trenika was independent in her own successful endeavors. Thanks to Kaedon's profitable trucking business. She could have her pieces distributed throughout the United States and even have pieces from potential artists shipped in through the same route to display in her gallery. Trenika was doing big things and her newfound title of being the new queen of contemporary art was accepted with grace. All she knew was love and art.

Trenika considered herself blessed beyond the dreams of a thousand women put together.

This evening her and Lisa were celebrating the anniversary of their friendship. Also present was Pooh Baby who eventually moved down to Atlanta two years ago. When he learned that Atlanta had become the new headquarters for the gay community, Pooh Baby wanted to relocate so he could live out his dreams of being a transgender female. Within a year and a half Pooh Baby was one of the top transgender models in the game. So, the three friends had more than a friendship anniversary to celebrate, because Pooh Baby was the face of his own gay magazine that sold its first 20,000 copies its first week. It was another win for the team. Sipping champagne and dressed to kill in her $1,800 cashmere Khaite sweater and $500 Tory Burch sandals, Trenika was feeling herself. She had more than enough eyes checking her out and knew it, but never would she attempt to entertain her many admirers. Niggas knew whose wife she was and if crossed, Kaedon was coming straight for their heads. From the streets to the boardroom, it was clear that Trnika was off limits, unless they wanted to be another dead body. She was the wife of a fearless gangsta who thought the world of her. But there would always be someone who considered themselves just as fearless and gangsta enough to try.

"Guess who?" Trenika felt a pair of hands cover her eyes from behind and smiled at the voice behind her ear that was altered but not unrecognizable.

"Sha'NayNay from Martin?" Guessed Trenika

"Bitch, you got me fucked up!" Naja pushed her in the back of the head and pulled up a chair and sat in it backwards. Dressed fresh to impress in her Gucci linen and a $6,300 Rick Owens jacket, Naja was now on top of her game in the streets.

"What's up, cuz?" Trenika gave Kaedon's cousin a high five and offered her a glass of champagne to celebrate.

"What's the occasion?" Asked Naja.

Trenika told her as she watched Naja pour herself a glass and saluted them with her drink.

"True friendship is worth everything," said Naja and toasted her glass with them all.

"And them coins too, baby!" Said Pooh Baby, dancing in his seat while dressed in a $590 Naked Princess gown and Pierre Hardy heels looking like a darker version of the artist Ella Mai: Already several people have mistaken him for a real bitch up in the lounge. Little did they know.

People like Pooh Baby were dangerous.

He was deadly. The nigga literally looked like a real deal woman.

"Is Kae in tonight?" Naja asked.

"You just missed him about fifteen minutes ago." Trenika looked at her and said. "Why? Is everything alright, Naja?" She wanted to know.

"Everything's kosher. I just wanted him to meet somebody."

"Who?" Said Trenika curiously

"Just a business associate of mine."

"I can call him for you." she suggested.

Naja shook her head and downed her drink. "No need. He'll have his chance sooner or later," she said. Then she got up and walked away from the table.

Trenika watched as Naja made her way across the lounge and took a seat at another table. There were two others occupying the table, both women and obviously important enough to be wearing such expensive clothing. One was black and beautiful, and the other a much older woman who appeared to be of Asian descent.

"What does Ms. Thang got going on now?" Pooh Baby said this with a hint of dismay in his voice.

"What she doesn't have going on," Frowned Lisa, frowning up her face. "Y'all heard about that foolishness she did at the Magic City strip club?"

"You talkin' about when that stripper got attacked and they broke her arms and legs? Who didn't hear about that bullshit? It was dead wrong what they did to that poor girl," said Pooh Baby.

"Word on the streets is that Milkshake owed Naja a lot of money and was playing games. So Naja paid her bitches to do that girl dirty right there in front of everybody while she stood there watching and laughing like the shit was funny."

"That's a cold bitch."

"Heartless," Lisa shook her head sadly. "But that's my girl, though. The bitch just got some mental problems."

Pooh Baby said, "What's wrong, Tee?"

All eyes swiveled over to Trenika who was still looking in Naja's direction across the room. There was something about the Asian woman that seemed so familiar to Trenika that she was trying to pinpoint but couldn't. Something about the woman struck her as oddly familiar but to an unsettling effect.

What was it about the woman that bothered her so?

Then as if she had read her thoughts, the Asian woman turned her gaze on Trenika and looked her dead in the eyes.

And that's when it registered.

Trenika couldn't believe her eyes. "Oh no," she muttered to herself.

And then she stood up and made her way across the room.

***

It was a cold January evening in the city of Atlanta. Kaedon pulled on his Brioni turtleneck sweater over his tan Thom Browne pants getting ready to go meet with his business partner about a breach of contract.

With the two rigs Kaedon owned he was contracted by a coastal lumber company down in north Florida that sent his driver all over the East Coast. This evening Kaedon was called by Frank to come to the truck yard immediately. When asked about the situation Kaedon was told there had been a breach of contract, which was an issue that he took seriously.

Timothy Andrews, the second driver of Kaedon's other rig, was way up in Chicago honoring another driving contract they had with the Ritz Carlton Hotel corporation. Then there was Wal-Mart as well, which was bringing in the money from both contracts. But here it was after four years of running a successful business, a situation has presented itself where one's license could be taken away from them. That's the last thing Kaedon needed was a situation like that where he could lose a good contract.

Checking the time on his Hermes watch and seeing that it was nearly 7:00 p.m., Kaedon received the call twelve minutes ago when he was taking it in for the evening. He wasn't planning on being out all night with whatever's going on.

There was a knock at the bedroom door.

"Daddy?" Aryanna was now tall and shapely for a ten-year-old, still beautiful and bright as ever, and very much more spontaneous than she was five years earlier. "Can Jade come over and sleepover with me since it's almost weekend?" She asked.

"Did you ask your mama?" The day was Thursday, thought Kaedon.

"I'm asking you," she said, smiling that winning smile of hers. "I think you should say yes, because her parents are having another house party tonight and that's not the type of environment for a child. You know, the drugs, drinking, violence…"

"Okay, Ary. You don't have to run that game on me," said Kaedon.

"So, she could come?" She asked.

"Do I have to go pick her up too?" he asked.

Aryanna grinned and looked behind her, stepping aside to allow little Jade to come rushing into the room. She threw her arms around her uncle Kaedon and thanked him for letting her stay over for the night.

Looking in Aryanna's direction, Kaedon shook his head as she tossed up the deuces at him before running off with her friend from down the street.

A minute later, he walked past Aryanna's bedroom door where her and Jade were inside giggling up a storm. He headed up the hallway of his stucco-styled five-bedroom house that he now owned out in Newnan, Georgia which was on the outskirts of Atlanta. He entered the spacious living room to find his son, Kahlil, stretched out on the floor in front of the TV watching Cartoon Network. Curled up on the sofa surfing the internet channels on her phone was Donecia, now a freshman at Spelman University and taking up babysitting duties to make some extra side money.

Years ago, while still in New Orleans, it was then that Trenika confessed to him about Jourdan and her family's situation. At first, Kaedon was angered by the predicament she had put them in by befriending the woman. But he eventually relented and accepted the new family into their lives. But not before making it clear to All that he didn't approve of him testifying against his colleagues, and so he convinced Al to do otherwise. Kaedon promised him that his family will be okay and so far, for the past four years since reclaiming their lives back after enduring a year of total legal bullshit, Al and his family decided to remain in Georgia as a new fresh start.

And that's how Donecia got into college there, going totally against the Ivy League colleges her father had prepared her for. Donecia was loving her new independence, and the girl had all the right to do so after living such a sheltered life.

"I won't be gone long," said Kaedon as he snatched up his jacket from the coat closet. "Just make sure Kahlil doesn't drink too much soda again tonight."

"I gotcha, Kae." Donecia didn't even look up from her phone.

"You said that last time. Dee." he retorted.

She looked up at him. "I can't help how much I adore his bad ass," said Donecia, resembling the actress Zendaya but with a little more thickness in the hips. "There's not much I wouldn't do for him if he asks."

"You need to be more disciplined towards him."

"I will," she promised.

"Whatever, Dee. Remember the ultimate rule," he told her.

"No boys in the house. Gotcha. Bye, Mr. Grouch."

"Shut up," Kaedon said before opening the door and letting himself out. Doneica was a very sweet and reliable girl, but Kaedon was not lost on her crafty nature to do things outside her boundaries.

He just prayed that her craftiness didn't one day cause him to lose all trust in her.

Chapter 15

Her name was Vivian Wu and she was now staring up at Trenika with a look of dismay on her face as she approached their table. In a discreet manner Vivian Wu shook her head at Trenika, but Trenika only shook her head no and kept right on walking her way. She was walking with a purpose.

Halfway there the entrance door to the lounge opened and two people entered the big room. One of them was Jourdon and behind her was a well-known street hustler she knew by Sonny Boy. Sonny Boy headed in her direction, but before he could reach her, the totally unexpected happened. Across the room at the table Naja was occupying, the woman sitting next to Vivian Wu, materialized with a Sig Sauer P938 pistol with a Dead Air Ghost silencer and aimed it at Naja's face. Trenika halted instantly as she watched the Asian woman turn back to Naja and said something to her. Moments later both women rose from the table and made way for the exit with Vivian Wu in the lead.

Sonny Boy had closed the distance between them and Trenika held up a patient hand at him to shush him. This was the young hustler that calls himself liking Donecia and put it in his mind that since he was cool with Kaedon, that he could use her to help him win Donecia over.

The nigga had the bland sense of a donkey.

He was pitifully in love with a girl who had no qualms about using him like the mark he was.

Turning away from Sonny Boy, Trenika stepped forward to confront the Asian woman. It's been years since she saw the older woman, but as she observed her now at that moment, Trenika could easily see that Vivian was still that same old vicious bitch she remembered.

"It's been a long time, Trenika. It's good to see you again despite the last time we met. I'm sorry you had to witness that a minute ago. But as you already know, business is always business with me, it's never personal," said Vivian.

"What's going on between you and my girl?"

"I think that's a question for your friend to answer to, Trenika."

Trenika said, "Is it something I can do to help?"

"Always the amiable one, you are. But no, Trenika. This is a matter that only Naja could prevent from happening. Have yourself a good evening, old friend. "With that being said, Vivian stepped around her and exited the building with her beautiful female assassin watching her back.

To the average eye one would expect both women to be just two normal people out on the town, not one of them being the niece of the man who happens to be the head honcho of the Asian mob. The same woman whose niece was Trenika's old friend from college that Trenika watched get kidnapped and later murdered because she disobeyed the laws of her family's strict regulations.

Her name was Hannah-Shiung Wu, and she was in love with a black guy. When Hannah married him against her family's wishes and was impregnated by him, Vivian was sent to execute her own niece to honor their royal bloodline. Hannah had become a disgrace to her family and paid a deadly price for her actions. So, if the woman would kill her own niece, there's no question what she would do to Naja if crossed.

Right then Trenika turned toward her husband's cousin and saw Naja lighting up a blunt, while still sitting down at the table as if she hadn't just got her life threatened.

That was Naja, always the calm, cool, collected one, never the type to show her truest feelings.

Trenika made her way over to the table and took a seat right across from Naja where Vivian had been sitting just a minute ago, "You mind telling me what the fuck was that about just now, Naja?" She demanded.

"What you saw doesn't concern you, Nika," said Naja.

"It does when you initially wanted my husband involved in it," she shot back evenly.

"I didn't expect it to go that far."

"Well it did and I wanna know why? You see, I know Vivian personally, and for a long time."

"Vivian?" Naja looked at her ambiguously.

"Yeah."

"She told me her name was Ava."

Trenika said, "her name is Vivian and she's with the Asian mob. The woman is a real killer and you need to be aware what type of people you're dealing with."

"She wants me to kill Miami Shane."

"What!" Trenika bellowed.

"She paid me a hundred bandz to do it and I've yet to find this nigga. I got all my girls out there lookin' for this nigga and he's nowhere to be found. When I wasn't lookin' for the nigga he was all over the place. Now it's like he knows he's living on borrowed time."

"If whatever he did to Vivian was worth him dying over, he knows, Naja. and you better believe he got people watching out for anything that's out of character."

"Of course."

"Which means they could be watching you too." Trenika saw the expression on Naja's face change from calm to a look of concern. The person whom they were talking about was a business tycoon hailed from South Miami to build his empire there in Atlanta. Miami Shane owned a record label, restaurants, and even a laundromat business throughout the state. But Miami Shane was a thoroughbred killer too one that the streets feared and hated altogether.

Naja knew this to be true but yet she chose to take a hit on a nigga that just might get her killed.

"But what I don't understand, Naja, is why the fuck did you want my husband to meet someone like that?"

Naja didn't answer.

She couldn't.

Kaedon warned her to never say a thing as to why he wanted to meet with Vivian Wu.

***

"This is what I found," said Frank Bittle, a big wide-shouldered white guy who looked more like a Viking than a truck driver with a bad case of bronchitis.

Kaedon, with the flashlight in hand, shone the light down into the bed of lumber, felt his pulse quicken.

Hours ago, while refilling at a truck stop down in Midway, Florida. Frank was ambushed by three armed goons. While one of them held him at gunpoint, the other two climbed up onto the bed of the truck of lumber. A retired weapon specialist and an Army veteran, it didn't take long for Frank to analyze his opponent for a plan of attack. After swiftly disarming the gunman and left him out cold on the ground, Frank went after the other two. He ended up having to shoot and kill one of them, the other one got away. When the cops arrived Frank only told them that they attempted to rob him, and he had to defend himself.

Afterwards, Frank drove to Atlanta and called Kaedon as soon as he located what the goons had been trying to find. Which was what they were both examining at that very moment.

"This isn't good," said Kaedon.

"Not good at all."

Kaedon reached into the hollow cove of one of the lumber twenty-foot logs and took up the shrink-wrapped packages inside. There was a total of ten packages inside. Whoever planted the drugs in a lumber of wood was good.

"Fuck it. I want every last one of these muthafuckerz checked for drugs. No exceptions. Somebody is fuckin' with my business and I'm gonna get to the bottom of it." said Kaedon.

"You want all this done tonight?" Frank asked.

"Tonight." He stated simply.

Frank gave him a look of uncertainty.

"Is there a problem, Frank?" Kaedon was so pissed that he wanted to break something. He had a feeling who might be responsible and that's who he going to confront.

"We have a total of two hundred and eighty logs here, Kaedon.

To check all of them tonight I would need the use of some heavy machinery. Where would I get that type of equipment at a time like this?"

He had a point, thought Kaedon.

"Okay. Leave it be for now. Where was your location originally, Frank?" Kaedon wanted to know.

"To Chapel Hill, North Carolina. The delay cut off half of my time, I would have gotten there by dawn. I think it'll be wise to just continue my route and unload there. By that time, you should have worked out the differences, right? I mean, wouldn't that be the best way?"

Kaedon thought about it for a moment and had to agree with Frank's insight. Whoever was behind the drugs lying at his feet right now either knew him personally to infiltrate his delivery routes, or they just didn't give a fuck and decided to manipulate the system of whoever they could use to traffic their product without anyone being the wiser.

What they probably didn't expect was for a team of guys attempting to rob the shipment of drugs at the risk of one dying and another getting locked up behind it. Whoever the third guy was, got lucky and escaped the fate that Frank was surely going to hand him.

"Finish your delivery, Frank. I'll take care of the rest," Kaedon told the man standing before him.

"Wise choice, Kaedon. I'm on it," Frank headed for the lounge building area of the truck yard location that Kaedon also owned. It was pretty much the same type of warehouse building that Amod had back over in New Orleans. Only difference is, Kaedon owns three of them where other truckers had a place to house and detail their rigs when it's needed.

Kaedon gathered up the ten packages contained in a Hefty trash bag that Frank brought out to him.

"I'll have something nice waitin' on you, Frank, when you get back in town. Thank you for what you did tonight. Your loyalty will not be forgotten." Kaedon hefted the bag over his shoulder like a man on a mission.

"I only did what I would want somebody to do for me, Kaedon." Frank replied in that southern drawl he had.

Kaedon nodded and went on his way.

Somebody had crossed the line, and he intended on making them pay for their mistake.

Chapter 16

Thirty minutes later Kaedon was seething like a mad hyena at Naja and her bullshit. When Trenika had called him demanding his presence, Kaedon stopped everything he was doing to go see to his wife. After hearing what Trenika had to say, she demanded that he tell her why Naja didn't want to explain his involvement.

Years ago, Trenika had told Kaedon about her friend Hannah and what was done to her. That conversation led to Lance overhearing it and his confessing to fucking Hannah without his sister knowing. Then about the older Asian woman proposing a business deal with him after she learned of his hustles and his connection to Trenika. Fulfilling Lance's hustler's dream by giving him a connect with her people was Vivian's way of compensation for the loss of a friend she had taken from his sister.

Being that Kaedon was out of the street game by then, he didn't want to entertain the thought of involvement. But ever since Lance and Naja first met they had kept in touch over the years. Until just a couple of years ago when Naja had visited New Orleans and Lance introduced her to Vivian. After she met the Asian woman Naja's hustle game soared, and of course she had to tell Kaedon all about it. Kaedon wasn't the groupie type, nor did he expect to do business with Vivian, all he wanted was to meet the woman whose touch turns everything to gold. But no way did he want

Trenika to find out that he had shared the company of the same woman who had murdered her friend back in college.

For so long now Lance and Naja had been keeping the truth of their involvement away from Trenika. But Naja's obviously stupid decision to invite Vivian to the lounge that evening at the risk of Trenika seeing her again was not smart.

And now Kaedon was mad like hell for having to explain to Trenika what was really going on. Although he knew nothing about the hit on Miami Shane, whom Kaedon admitted he knew and respected, it still left him flabbergasted that Naja even agreed to take the hit. He didn't doubt that she could kill Miami Shane, what bothered him is the fact that he thought her and him were tight.

Was the money making his cousin disloyal? Wondered Kaedon as he made his way to his home study.

Trenika had gotten so pissed with him that she kicked him out the bedroom to be alone. Eventually she'll find her way outside into the pool house where she remodeled into her workshop for painting. It was moments like this where she would go in and leave out with a masterpiece.

She was raw like that.

It didn't bother Kaedon none because he had some work to do that he had put off for too long.

Sitting behind the big mahogany desk in his home office, Kaedon unlocked the side drawer with a small key he kept hidden beneath one of the back legs of the desk. Inside the drawer he retrieved a smartphone that was only used for discreet purposes unlike his personal line of communication. Kaedon needed some answers, and he wanted them as soon as possible.

"Brah, what the hell do you want? I was just on the phone with this old freak bitch. You lucky I fucks with your raggedy ass or I'll still be tryna get grandma to bust that old pussy for me."

"What's going on, Qay?" Kaedon smirked.

"What it do, pimp!" Qay Bradwell was Amod's cousin, Baby gal's baby daddy, that Amod had recently reconnected with. Qay was also Nardo and Vega's first cousin whom they left for dead facing two murder charges up in Tallahassee after blasting on some southside niggas at the car show years ago. Now back in the county on another murder after beating the first two, Qay said, "I was hoping you call, though."

"What's up, Qay?"

"Do you know some young nigga they call Skip from over out of Lake Skillet area?"

"Toya brotha, Skip? Yeah. I know him. Why?"

"Just checking the trap," said Qay. "The lil' nigga in here on a pistol case. He tryna get down with the fellaz and used your name as a reference, that's all."

Kaedon knew Skip very good. Skip was a young nigga who was always begging the older hustlers for a shot. He used to run errands for Twan all the time. He turned out to be a good dude, but Skip had had a hard life just like the rest of them coming up in the streets.

"Give the lil' nigga a shot, brah. He'll handle his weight. But listen, I need some quick intel on a situation, Qay."

"Talk to me, my nigga."

Outside the office door the sound of Aryanna and Jade chasing Kahlil down the hallway caught Kaedon's attention. The girls always teased Kahlil, but when he teaed them back they didn't like his methods of payback.

"Brah, I think there's a guy that came to county a few hours ago for robbery, or an attempt. But one of his men got murked in the process—" Kaedon was saying.

"At the Flying Jays Truck Stop in Midway? Yeah." Qay cut in.

"So, you know?" Kaedon paused.

"The nigga is from out there in Havana somewhere. I think they call him Eddie Geez or something. Yeah. That's him."

"I need you to squeeze him for me. It was one of my rigs they tried to rob. They had come to collect something and I wanna know who sent them and why."

"Say no more," Qay's voice had lowered to that tone that was only meant for something grave.

"I need that done like yesterday, my nigga.

"Why are we still talking, pimp?" Qay disconnected. From tehre Qay would gather up his team and give them the rundown on what the play was. There was a possibility that Eddie Geez won't lie to see tomorrow, but Kaedon couldn't car less if he don't, all he want is a name.

The name of the muthafucker who crossed the line by running drugs through his legitimate business.

A total violation of protocol.

A deadly one.

***

Zamon had just finished eating a late dinner when he heard about the shooting in Midway, Florida. The story was all over social media as that of everything else. When he learned that the incident took place at a truck stop it made him think of his twin. He knew all about Kaedon's trucking business and the coincidence just made him wonder. Since his own shooting incident which had led him to be confined to a wheelchair for the rest of his life, Zamon had been spared a lifelong phase of self-hate. Though the first couple of years in and out of surgeries and physical therapies were so tiring he just wanted to give up on life. But people like Kaedon, Tazzy, his wife and son, were a constant reminder just how important life was to him. Kaedon had become a staple of support to him and his family, so much so that Zamon was pretty much forced by his twin brother to make something out of his life. The situation was so surreal that failure was not an option for Zamon.

Gradually as his strength in heart became his motivation, and that motivation became a daily reminder of how powerful he still was despite his predicament, Zamon became that force to be reckoned with. He eventually went back to teaching and reclaimed his position in life of being the proud father of a tough little boy who never ceased to amaze him.

In the last five years since the shooting, Zamon could actually say that he hadn't been so focused in his life. He learned to accept his disability early on and embraced all the challenges that life tossed in his path along the way. And boy was there some very heartfelt challenges he had to endure. Some he still found particularly worrisome where his wife Melody was concerned. There was no doubt in his mind that she still loved him, it was the life she now lived that she didn't love. Zamon felt the only reason why she hadn't left already was for the sake of their baby boy and her guilty conscience of leaving him to fend for himself. She wasn't happy anymore, they couldn't do the things that they used to do. They argued a lot now more than ever, and even that has taken a turn for the worse. It was as though Melody was looking for a reason to argue, so she could run off and do God knows what. His marriage was slowly falling to pieces now, and Zamon wondered how long it would be before it's finally over.

Having Melody leave him because she couldn't handle the pressure of being married to a cripple was scary. But who is he to stop her if she does go? It's not like he could go chasing after her if she did.

Zamon knew his marriage was over when Melody began to complain about their sex life and how his eating her pussy and him using a dildo on her just wasn't cutting it anymore. Melody was not satisfied, and her womanly needs had become a serious problem at home.

Shaking off the painful reality of his thoughts, Zamon wheeled himself into his home study. There he poured himself a glass of Brandy and downed all of its contents before refilling his glass. Then with that same glass he wheeled over to the desk. This is where he spent most of his evening going over homework and preparations for what he wanted to present the following attendance.

He decided to call and check on his twin brother.

"How I knew you would call?" Kaedon said the instant he answered the phone.

"Any reason why you figured I would?"

"You tell me, brah."

And told him Zamon did, stressing what he learned on social media that very evening.

"I'm good, Zee. How about you? What do you got going on this weekend?"

"Work-work-work, bro."

"Too much work can get in the way of family time, my nigga," said Kaedon with a chuckle.

"And that's the point of me working, Kaedon." Zamon closed his eyes and sighed. "I'm going through it, man. I don't know what else to do." He said.

"Melody?" Kaedon asked.

"Yes," he answered. "I think it's over, bro." And then Zamon poured his heart out to the only person he feel he could trust with his fears.

Chapter 17

Naja parked the burgundy Chevy Tahoe beneath a Crepe Myrtle tree a block away from the address one of her girls had given her. Despite the weak sunshine filtering through the high, thin clouds, it was dim and cold inside the truck. Naja turned on the heater system. The warm air that began blowing through the vents smelled like scorched dust.

Laura Boyd's house looked exactly like all the others. Despite the cold fear in her gut and the serrated blade of her conscience that was cutting into her heart, Naja wondered if what she had been told was true. That Laura Boyd was Miami Shane's godmother who had relocated there from Tampa, Florida many years ago. It's also said that Miami Shane frequents the home of his godmother in the mornings to check up on her and make sure her life was in order.

The house was only two rooms wide, but deep, so that the back porch was almost even with the alley behind the house. It had been painted at one time, though now that greenish paint was a distant memory. The yellowish tarpaper roof was patched and peeling. The metal chimney had rusted and left a brown stain bleeding down the exterior wall. From the outside, it appeared that no one was home. Heavy shades had been pulled over all the windows.

What Naja didn't understand was why Miami Shane had his godmother living so poorly with all the money he was making in the streets. The nigga was literally on kingpin status and yet his godmother was not properly well off.

Suddenly, the ring of her cellphone snapped Naja out of her thoughts. She reached for her phone and saw that it was Kaedon calling. At the sight of his number Naja automatically knew this wasn't going to be good. She looked forward to his call the night before, but he never called.

"Hello?" She tried to keep her voice even.

"You need to get here, cuz. I'm at Burn One. I don't give a fuck what you doing right now. I need to see you." Kaedon sounded fierce and it made her recoil at the tone in which he used with her.

"Okay," she told him. "I'm coming."

"Now, Ranaja."

When he called her by her full name, she knew that Kaedon was graveyard serious.

Naja took one more longing look towards the house and shook her head. She started the engine of the truck and headed back across town. Naja wasn't afraid of her cousin or anything, she just didn't want to deal with him confrontationally.

It didn't take Naja long to make it to her Burn One Smoke Shop. When she did, she noticed Kaedon's Lexus UX coupe parked out front among the rest of the cars. She got out of the truck just as Kaedon was exiting the shop. In his hand,he carried a takeout bag from Arby's Restaurant. Kaedon signaled for her to get back in the truck and she did. The look on his face didn't match the tone in which he used earlier. But Kaedon wasn't the emotional type. He was always the humbled type of guy. He was always calm under pressure.

Back in the truck, Naja watched as Kaedon approached and slid into the seat beside her.

"What's up, cuz?"

"You mind tellin' me what the fuck is this?" Kaedon said as he reached into the bag and tossed its contents onto her lap, sneering darkly and now obviously furious.

Naja looked down at the shrink-wrapped package in her lap and picked it up. "It's a kilo of heroin," she said.

Kaedon had been watching her closely and trying to gauge her reaction. "I know it's fuckin' heroin, Naja but what the fuck was it doing on one of my truck routes?"

"What do you mean?" She asked.

He seethed at her. "That shit was hidden in one of the loads on my truck," said Kaedon. Then he went on to tell her about what Frank had to go through to discover it.

"Oh shit, cuz. I heard about that shit this morning." Naja was shocked by this news. She examined the package and thought it looked familiar. Although she wasn't into the drug trade anymore, she still kept a few people in pocket who does. "Wait a minute, Kae," she muttered. "I think I know whose product this is."

"All I need is a name," he said.

Without saying a word, Naja restarted the engine and backed out of the parking space. The look on her face was grim, her eyes were ice cold, and her heart, not right. Where she was going, Naja was about to really get on some gangsta shit.

She felt crossed too.

Shit was about to turn the fuck up.

***

Ciera was in the office printing out some paperwork standing before the copy machine when her boss peeped her head in and called out to her.

"Ms. Crawford, you have a call on line one with Shank's Middle," said Evelyn Rich, the Senior Director of the Gadsden County School Board and Ciera's mentor.

"Okay. Thanks, Eve," Ciera whispered and automatically knew what the call was about. It had to be in regards to her son Malik, who has become quite a problem in school lately. Twelve years old and hardheaded, always cynical about other people's motives, and quite vicious towards his peers to say the least.

Ciera left the records room office for her office which was adjacent to the main front office. She shut the door behind her and slid around to the back of her desk. Lifting the black phone off her desk and pressing the blinking red button for line one, Ciera anticipated the troubling news she was about to hear.

"Hello. This is Ms. Ciera Crawford."

"Good morning, ma'am. This is principal Shannon Davis here at Shanks Middle school. I'm calling in regard to your son Malik. Apparently, he's been selling the schoolkids here cigarettes and a confrontation with another student transpired from it. Malik has physically assaulted one of the students and a backpack full of cigarettes was confiscated from him. As of today your son is suspended for approximately ten days, along with two weeks of detention for his behavior," said the school's principal.

"Is my son still present right now?"

"Yes, he is," said Principal Davis.

Last time Malik was suspended from school, he demanded his walking papers and then took it upon himself to walk home. Ciera had caught up to her son halfway there to the house and gave him a mean verbal thrashing. Malik was really getting out of control.

She told the principal that she was on her way to pick him up. When she went to her boss for a moment to inform her on what was going on, Evelyn Rich shooed her off and told her that she understood.

That was another thing that she hated about Malik's situation. His behavioral pattern has become something like a legend around the office. By now everybody knew she had a troublesome child and that alone made her feel awful. Malik didn't have a positive male figure in his life, and Ciera believed that had something to do with his behavior.

It was situations like these when Ciera just wanted to send him off to his Uncle Kaedon. If there was one person who will get his mind straight it would be Kaedon. Her little brother wasn't going to play with his ass. Malik needed tougher love in his life.

Figuring he was too old for ass whippings, Ciera wanted him to experience a whole other type of discipline. In another week, Malik would be thirteen years old, which meant that all that little boy shit needed to cease.

A block away from the school, Ciera saw that he had walked off the school premises once again. She caught him shooting across the street of Pat Thomas over to the KFC restaurant. She honked the car horn and hit the blinkers to make the turn into the entrance of the chicken joint. Malik turned to look at her over his shoulder. Their gazes met for a brief instant and then he moved towards the passenger door.

When her son slid into the seat next to her, Malik extended the walking papers toward her.

"I don't want that shit, Malik. I want to know when are you gonna get your fuckin' act together?" She snapped on him as she proceeded to take him home.

As she was delivering him a tongue lashing that he had grown accustomed to already, Malik reached into his pants pocket to which he pulled out a thick know of bills. When Ciera saw all the money she had to do a double take, as the worst thing her son could have done for money like that burned her heart with absolute dread.

Malik located her purse and deposited the money directly inside.

"What's that for?" Ciera caught herself saying.

"I don't see nobody else doing anythang to help out, mama," said Malik. "I hear how you be complaining on the phone to Aunt Takeya and Pam about bills and everythang. I figured I could help by doing what I can, mama. How do you think all that other money been mysteriously placed in your pocketbook? Or the money you found under your pillow? Or the money you found in your favorite shoes? Oh. I see, you thought it was Jerrod doing it the whole time." Malik snorted a wicked laugh. "That chump couldn't even afford to take you out to a nicer place to eat than at Olive Garden. You deserve better than that, mama. You deserve to be more content in life than you are now."

Ciera was in tears as she heard him out, never for one moment believing he even felt that way.

"So, before you start judging me and condemning me for the things I did to get suspended," Malik spoke up again. "Think about why I made the choice to do it in the first place. I love you, mama, and I'm here for you."

"I love you too," she sobbed. "I love you so much."

"Now, stop crying." Malik reached over to wipe the tears away from her beautiful face.

When Ciera finally made it to her house in the driveway, she turned to her son and no longer saw a child there. All this time Malik had been putting in work and taking care of the family without anyone being the wiser.

"My little black sheep," she said as she reached for Malik and pulled him into her arms.

"Only for you, mama," Malik answered proudly.

"I know," Ciera said with pride swelling in her heart. "I know this without a shadow of doubt."

Chapter 18

Fridays were the days that Kelly visited her man's father at the Hope & Grace Senior Housing Facility. It was one of things Chad made her promise. That no matter what, she would look after his father. And for nearly ten years now, Kelly has made solid on that promise. Chad's father was eighty-two years old now and barely hanging on.

So if they wanted to catch Kelly, there would be no better time to do it than at that moment.

Naja suspected her friend the instant it was said that the packages were hidden onto one of Kaedon's truck loads. It was the initial business arrangement that she had wanted her and Kaedon to discuss when she brought them together years ago. Although the method that was used to move the product wasn't Kelly's style, Naja was only aware of other performances.

Kaedon was plotting on how he was going to deal with Kelly without going through all the extra bullshit he didn't want to do. He wanted blood for his respect, though.

While bouncing around scenarios in which he was planning to execute, Kaedon was not expecting a call from Amod at that very moment.

"I got cuz on the line with me, my nigga," said Amond when Kaedon answered the phone.

"Yo!" Came Qay's voice a second later. "What it do, pimp?"

"I don't know, brah. You tell me."

Kaedon had a really bad feeling about this phone call. He had been anticipating Qay's call all morning, but figured he couldn't take care of his end yet if he hadn't called.

"Shit got messy this morning at breakfast time, and they had to put the block on lockdown. That's why I couldn't hit you up earlier, pimp. Shit was fucked up—"

"Nigga, I don't give a fuck about all that shit." Kaedon cut Qay off, anxiously wanting the information that he so desired to know." Tell me what I need to know, Qay."

"Lenny Baker."

"Huh?" Did Kaedon actually hear him right?

Qay repeated the name and Kaedon felt himself beginning to boil with dark rage.

"And that pussy muthafucker that got away? That was that bitch made nigga Rico Green. It's his brotha Mike-Mike who put everything together. Mike-Mike takes his orders from Lenny, and Rico doubles back to rob the shipment. Word is the two brothaz were beefing over something and that's why the shit even went down," said Qay.

"It's been confirmed, my nigga. I did my own homework on the matter and everything cuz said checked out." Amod's word was credible and so Kaedon knew now where he needed to direct his awakened ravenous appetite for blood.

They were pulling up into the parking lot out front of the senior citizen home facility.

"I'll handle it from here," Kaedon replied.

"I can slide on the first thang smoking out there right now," said Amod, ready to create tragedy.

"I got it, Amod."

"You sure?"

"Who am I, my nigga?" Kaedon stated and the silence that met him in response was an answer understood.

To question his ability to administer his gangsta when the time permits itself was like shooting yourself in the foot. It was stupid. Kaedon was a one-man army and by any means necessary he was about to show up and show out. He was back again like he never left.

"So, what're we doing?" Naja spoke up finally while looking over at her cousin with big hazel eyes of anxiousness.

"Kelly just got spared," he said.

"How so?" She asked.

He told her what he knew and all Naja could do was drop her head and release a long breath of relief. Because her and Kelly were friends, and she would have hated to see that friendship get tarnished by disloyalty. But the way things had looked a minute ago, Kelly was a dead bitch walking and there was not a damn thing she could do to stop it.

The gods were with her today.

Kelly was blessed.

***

Trenika busied herself preparing for the upcoming art show she was hosting at Prolific Arts Gallery of Contemporary Art Museum, which was her own establishment and her pride and joy. Trenika was excited about what was going to take place tomorrow afternoon. This was sure to be one of her biggest events yet.

Just the day before, Trenika had had pieces flown in by a representative of George Morrison, one of the nation's late greatest artists and a founding figure of Native American modernism. To display such art by such a respectable painter and sculptor was an honor like never before. Trenika had displayed pieces of other great artists but none like George Morrison, whose art she had grown to admire ever since she knew how to utilize a paint brush. There were people coming from as far as London to grace their presence in the event.

With the help of her team, which consisted of three arts majoring students, Aryanna's former art teacher Olivia Rowe, whom Trenika had eventually befriended, and four more loyal workers who never complained. The event was guaranteed to be a success. Trenika had worked damn hard for this opportunity, and she planned to bask in the glory.

Mommy was doing big things in the world, Aryanna would say when bragging about her mother's success. Baby girl was her biggest supporter ever.

It felt damn good to be doing something you love to do while getting paid for doing it. There was no better way to earn your keep.

"Mrs. Smith?" A voice called out.

Trenika turned from the large landscape painting by George Morrison to her newest recruit, Apryl Joiner. This was her twenty-one-year-old protege whom Trenika had met at one of her prior events. Apryl was delightful and sharp, and beheld a keen eye for detail when it came to art.

"Yes, Apryl?" she answered politely.

"There's a gentleman in the lobby requesting your presence, ma'am," Apryl told her. She was a very petite young woman with amazing gray eyes and a unique smile.

"Okay. I'll be there shortly," said Trenika before gazing down at the clipboard in her hand and jotting something down on the paper. One more look up at the landscape painting, Trenika shook her head in astonishment. She still could not believe that she was in possession of one of George Morrison's original paintings.

In the front lobby minutes later, Trenika was once again stunned by what lay before her eyes. The man that stood in her presence was another blast from her past. But this time, one whom she knew to be the chapter to a book that she vowed never to revisit again.

"Matthew." Trenika felt herself go numb with fear and sudden apprehension. "What a surprise," she replied. "To what do I owe this unexpected visit?"

That's when Matthew Wu closed the distance between them and took her hand into his. Then he hit her with that killer smile that his dear sister Hannah had always warned her about. The same smile that eventually and efficaciously persuaded her to do things that her tender heart couldn't deny.

"How about a lunch date?" He suggested.

"I'm married, Matt." She held up her diamond ring.

"Then consider it a business lunch." Matthew insisted and watched Trenika pause to think about it.

That was all it took for Trenika to think about it.

Hook, line, sinker.

Chapter 19

Malik waited until he heard the car reverse out of the gravel driveway before making his next move.

If he hadn't spazzed out today on Deon Washington about his money, his mother would have never known his secret. For almost two years now, Malik has been dabbling in street affairs, and hustling cigarettes to school kids was his thing. Kids nowadays were so smart they were dumb, and Malik was using their ignorance to his benefit. Nowadays kids were audacious and curious, and so covetous that they want to be like the more popular individuals just to try to be down. And smoking cigarettes away from home around those who encouraged them was so exciting to them.

Their desire to be hip was very beneficial for Malik. The hustle was so sweet that Malik manipulated the trust of the other kids in the form of a promise of secrecy. One of them was even paying him five dollars for just one cigarette. How could Malik not take advantage of such a situation?

The issue with Deon Washington, who was a seventh grader and what some may deem a bully, Malik secured an alliance with him for the greater good. Deon was to use his bully mentality to scare other school kids into buying cigarettes from him provided by Malik. After coming back short with his money twice, Malik decided to make an example out of Deon. He did it right in front of the whole school so every student could see who the real boss was.

Malik didn't want to do it, but something had to be done. Deon endured two blackeyes, a split lip, busted nose, and most importantly, a bruised ego.

After watching his mother's car drive away, Malik backed away from the living room window and headed down the hallway to his bedroom. Malik jumped off the porch into the streets a year ago, but his independent cigarette hustle came into existence a little longer than that. He was the black sheep of his family; one whose dream was to prevent his mother from having to need for anything.

In his bedroom, Malik marched over to his closet where he kept all his old shoes hidden in the back in shoe boxes. It was an old pair of Air Jordans he got for Christmas three years ago from his Uncle Kaedon. Stuffed inside the left shoe was a thick roll of money. Malik unbound the roll of cash of its rubber band and peeled off several bills he needed. After giving his mother the money earlier, that left his pockets tapped out. So now he must have pocket money and payment for what he had in mind to do.

Back at school, he had had his whole stash of cigarettes taken by the principal. For twenty dollars, he paid another badass kid who was in for skipping class to steal the backpack full of cigarettes back. Once he had reclaimed his product back, Malik decided to take his leave then. He couldn't remain on the campus as long as he had that backpack.

Malik was too smart for his own good. He knew this but his desire to hustle was too empowering to ignore.

He had heard all the stories about his Uncle Kaedon and his right hand man Twan. Niggas still was talking about Murda-K out there in the streets, and with those discussions came with a respect that Malik took with pride. He wanted to one day share that same love and respect that his uncle had in the streets. One that Kaedon, whether he respected it or not, would see that his determination was without fear of flaw. Malik wanted to make his uncle proud. He was next in line.

Fifteen minutes later, Malik knocked on the front door of a nearby house around the corner from where he lived. This was his road dawg, Junior's house. Someone he'd grown up with in the hood. Junior was two and a half years older than him, but between the two of them age didn't matter. They were road dawgs just how Kaedon and Twan were.

The front door opened, and a female stood there staring out at Malik. She was thick, fine with flawless caramel skin.

"What's up, M-Money?" Greeted Leah, seventeen years old and cool as a fan on a summer day.

"What's up, Leah?" He replied and entered the home of the person whom he trusted like a brother.

Upon entering the house Malik recognized two other guys besides Junior occupying the living room. One of them Malik knew as Rashad, was from around the Key Street Park but had moved to the High Bridge area of Quincy. The other kid Malik didn't know personally but had seen him around. Junior stepped out from the kitchen and the two road dawgs greeted each other with a fist bump and a brotherly hug.

This was Malik's ace for real. The same nigga who embraced him when he had nothing.

"Got some sacks left?" Malik pulled out his money.

"You know I keep that pressure, my nigga. But your money ain't buying shit from me, M-Money. You my brotha," Junior said with emphasis, glancing in the direction of the other two guys smoking weed on the sofa. Junior was the weed man in the hood, well one of them, but his business was booming good for a young nigga.

"I just want to support the hustle. That's all."

"Nigga, we eat from the same table. I don't know how many times I have to tell you that."

Malik nodded and put his money back in his pockets. "I need one to blow right now after what I had to go through this morning." He stressed.

"Got suspended from school again?" Junior asked.

He nodded. "Once again"

But it was all so worth it, Malik thought to himself and told his friend all about it.

***

Trenika would really be pissed at him if she knew of the arsenal of weapons that he kept hidden behind a secret wall panel of his home gym out back behind the house. But even more, Trenika would be boisterously livid with Kaedon if she knew what he was about to do.

And that's why he was choosing the SCAR 16S rifle and the Ruger Sniper's rifle with the 3x9 variable scope. That way he could hit his targets from a thousand yards and not have to get too deep in the field of war.

Kaedon wasn't going there to talk things out, he wanted to put an end to the whole situation. He knew all about Lenny Baker and where he came from. They had grown up together but lived on two opposite sides of town. Where Kaedon grew up in the Pepper Hill area, Lenny made his way up from East Quincy. Growing up in the same town, both men indulged in the same things but didn't share the same views of the game. Kaedon earned his keep by getting it from the mud and hustling to build his respect in the streets. But Lenny, all he did was rob, stole, and cutthroat his own people out to make a living.

There was no honor amongst thieves.

But Lenny eventually got his money up and was now doing big things in the area. Word was Lenny had been suspected in the death of his grandfather to earn the life insurance policy that was beneficial to him. Lenny being the only child and with his father overdosing when he was six years old, that left him to claim the $210,000 that was left to him along with his grandfather's house after he died.

Kaedon had no doubt in his mind that Lenny was responsible for the death of his grandfather, so that he could receive the money. That was the ultimate come up for a snake like Lenny to play a part in and benefit from. The shit was sad. It was a disgrace to his family.

That was four years ago and surprisingly, Lenny utilized his money and hustle game and became one of Quincy's most valuable players in the drug trade.

Kaedon was about to stop him once and for all. But first he needed to call his wife and inform her on the trip he needed to make back home.

He called Trenika's phone.

"Hello, baby. What's up?" She answered.

"What's up? Hey, I gotta go back home for a minute."

"What? Why? Is everything alright at home?" Trenika sounded genuinely concerned about the fact that her husband was going back home. "How long will you be gone?" She asked.

"Everything's good. It's all business. I'll only be gone for a day or two. You know I gotta check up on the old man while I'm there," he replied when he was climbing behind the wheel of his old Lincoln Aviator truck. He didn't want Naja tagging along and told her to just keep him updated on her groundwork of information she was good at.

"Okay," Trenika said slowly. "You got everything you need, Kae?" She asked.

Kaedon smirked as he started up his truck. "Everything except for some of that honey love you got me hooked on."

"It'll be right here when you get back," she said in that sexy way he loved. "Wet and ready," she added.

"It better be. I love you, beautiful." Kaedon vowed.

"I love you more," she sang.

I know, Kaedon thought to himself as he put the truck in gear. He knew Trenika loved him more than any woman has ever loved him. That's why he was making this move, because he couldn't allow anybody to jeopardize their futures by selfishly forcing their hand. Lenny had crossed the wrong nigga. He was dead.

Chapter 20

Trenika hung up the phone with her husband and looked across the table at Matthew Wu. She had agreed to go to lunch with him. They were dining out at the local Outback Steakhouse which was Trenika's favorite place to eat. She went against the more luxury diner that Matthew had suggested and chose the location she wanted.

The look on Matthew's face was one of silent curiosity, especially now after figuring out what the conclusion of Trenika's conversation with her husband was.

She ducked her head shyly.

"Nice. Love is a powerful thing," said Matthew.

His statement made her regard him with obvious refute. "What do you know of love, Matt?"

Matthew was an Asian of average height and weight, but a man of wealth and influence. At thirty-nine, Matthew has seen the world twice, and his knowledge in many cultures of life was remarkable. The man was nothing less than charming.

"Rather you believe it or not, Trenika, love has played a part of my world for the past two years," he said.

"Who is she?" Trenika smirked.

Matthew smiled. "Her name is Amelia. I met her three years ago in New York while scoping out a new place on the Upper East side of Manhattan. Instead of showing me nice homes to live in, I was thinking of better places for us to grow our family in. A year later after being friends, I'd decided to go another step further."

"Marriage?" A surprised look appeared on her face.

A sour look etched his. "Hell no!"

"But marriage is a lovely thing to have, Matt. Ever since Kaedon and I married my life has been nothing but blooming roses," said Trenika

"And that's what scares me, Trenika," he replied, and continued.

"How long will those roses stay blooming before their petals begin to fall away and die?"

She nodded solemnly. "A rose never actually dies, Matt. It creates life in others."

"I guess we'll see when we cross that bridge," Matthew replied when their food arrived.

They accepted their food and had their drinks refilled. Trenika told him the importance of prayer before placing a spread napkin onto her lap and bowed her head. She closed her eyes and blessed her food. When she reopened her eyes, Matthew was staring at her with interest.

"Eat your food, Matt." She dug into hers.

"Right." He blushed and began cutting into his rare steak.

For a minute they ate in silence before Trenika looked back up at him questioningly. "So why are you here in Atlanta?" She asked.

"My grandmother."

Trenika parsed momentarily. "I saw her yesterday evening at the lounge my husband owns."

"The Funny Bone," he stated. "Nice establishment."

"Yes," she noticed something flicker behind Matthew's eyes that made her wonder what that meant.

Another awkward silence ensued.

The story behind Matthew and his grandmother's beef transpired from the death of his sister. Matthew was angered by the decision that was made to kill Hannah. Back then it was a necessary thing to do given where they came from and how severely important it was to keep their bloodline pure. To banish Hannah from their family's royalties would have been good with Matthew, because he still would have been there for his sister. But to kill her instead created a hatred in his heart for his grandmother that made him stand up to her for the first time ever in his life.

Not only had Matthew relinquished his place in the family's empire, but he used the family's businesses to build his own empire. Where the family was focusing on doing away with the drug trade, Matthew encouraged it and built his own drug empire. And to upset his grandmother more, he had developed drug enterprises throughout the whole East Coast where some of her businesses were being compelled to oblige to his demands. Anything to make Vivian Wu wish that his father was still alive to stop him.

He had become a thorn in her side. He was a threat.

"Vivian is trying to shut down my Atlanta operation and I'm here to stop her," Matthew said with a sneer.

"Stop her, how? That's one of the most powerful women I know," Said Trenika.

"This has been an ongoing beef between her and I since…" he paused when Trenika shook her head, pleading with her pretty eyes for him not to say it. Matthew swallowed and shifted in his seat. "She'd had two of my biggest businesses shut down in New Jersey, four in South Carolina, one in Miami, and even one in Orlando. Here in Atlanta she is going after my prize investment –"

"Miami Shane?" She said.

He went suddenly still and gazed across the table at her in open astonishment. "You know."

"Of course I know. Vivian is using a very good friend of mine to carry out the hit. She came into the lounge yesterday evening threatening to kill my friend if she doesn't do it before the weekend is out," Trenika said, fuming.

"How much did she pay your friend?"

"A hundred thousand."

Matthew could only shake his head. "This friend of yours," he spoke up. "How good is she, Trenika?"

"Damn good. And I don't want nothing to happen to her behind this mess."

"Nothing won't," he promised her.

"I wish I could believe that, Matt."

"You can." Matthew reached across the table and took her by the hand. "Because if she's as good as you say she is, then a million dollars to take Vivian out of her misery would solve both our problems."

Trenika couldn't believe what she had just heard. A million dollars?" Just to kill Vivian Wu? She was considering doing it her gotdamn self!

***

Back at his road dawg's house, Malik was halfway down his blunt of weed when Junior sent his girlfriend Leah to bring him to the back of the house. He had been in his zone listening to Boston Richie booming from the sound system and thinking about all types of shit.

Junior's mother was a known crack addict by the name of Freaky Fran, and who was currently doing county time for a list of petty crimes. So him having the house to himself to pretty much do whatever he chose to do was a normal thing to him. He would take in youngsters like himself who be skipping school to give them a spot to chill. Junior was well loved and respected by the youngsters. He was the one that some of them wished they were or had it made like him. Junior loved his freedom to do whatever the fuck he wanted without having to answer to no one. He was a young king in a sense. An influencer.

Malik got up and followed Leah out of the room while staring at her apple bottom. She had a nice ass, and it jiggled without effort. Malik was very much into girls but didn't take them seriously.

There was only one girl that his young heart has been doting on since day one. She was a girl he was willing to wait for, no matter how long it took him. Although his family might not approve of his decision, Malik knew that this particular girl would. Until then, he would do his best to maintain his hustle and secure the bag, because when he made his move he wanted her to see that he could provide for her with the lifestyle she desired. Malik was willing to earn her heart. He was dedicated.

Junior was in his bedroom with a cigar box sitting on his lap and counting the stack of money he had piled next to him before binding each stack and securing it into the box. He looked up at Malik as he entered the room and told Leah to give them some privacy.

Leah left without a word. She was a loyal young bitch, and Junior would kill about her. He's already done it.

"I need to tell you something, lil' brah," said Junior, gesturing toward the bean bag chair next to the bed.

Malik sat down while still smoking on his solo blunt. He wanted to put it out and save the other half for later, but the weed was too good to save.

"What I'm about to tell you is facts. What you do afterwards is your choice. Just know that I got your back till the end."

Junior counted out the last stack and stored it into the box. No reply from Malik. But he did stub the blunt out for later. He was all ears.

You can feel the change of atmosphere.

"That little nigga up there, Fonzo? Rashad has been bringing the lil' nigga around here for the last few days. But not only is the nigga Fonzo a thief-Leah caught the slick muthafucka stealing shit from between the cushions on the sofa – but he's also a threat to your Uncle Kaedon."

That caught Malik's attention. "He's what?"

And that's when Junior told him about the incident between Kaedon and Vega, which led to Kaedon running down on Lonzo, who was Fonzo's father, and made him snitch on his men before killing himself that very same night.

"It was his old boy's birthday yesterday and his people always did something on Lonzo's birthday." Junior looked over at Malik and saw the fury raging in his eyes. "Apparently he just learned the real truth about what happened to his father, but he doesn't know that you are Kaedon's nephew. That night your uncle slapped that nigga down up there and that's something one would never forget," he finished.

Malik rose up to his feet. "Thank you for the heads up, Junior," he replied.

"Whatever you decide to do I'm with you," he said. Junior stood up next, moving over to stand in front of Malik and put a hand on his shoulder. "You can't sleep on a lil' nigga like that, M-Money. If he'd stab his own auntie in her sleep, what you think he'll do to you? He just spent a year in juvie behind that shit."

"I know what to do."

"You sure?"

Malik nodded. "I guess it's time to make him bleed."

"Okay. Then let's get to it, my nigga."

Chapter 21

Malik walked up from the back of the house into the living room where he found Leah curled up on the sofa flipping through the TV channels looking for something to watch. Neither Fonzo nor Rashad was occupying the room where they had been just minutes ago.

"Where they went?" Asked Malik.

"I told them to get out," she replied. "All they wanna do is sit up in here and smoke weed all day and tryna look between a bitch's legs." Leah added.

Junior entered the room behind Malik while tucking his .380 automatic pistol into his front pocket.

Without a word, Malk reached into Junior's front pocket for the pistol and told him to just watch his back. Then, he headed for the front door and exited at once.

Outside Fonzo and Rashad were seen walking down the sidewalk up ahead about twenty yards off.

Malik hurried off the porch and hit the sidewalk behind them. He wasn't scared of what he was about to do, but he was nervous about what his mother would do. Because there was only one way to justify what he was about to do when the police showed up afterwards. Malik was very smart for his age; he was way too clever and cunning to not get away with what he was planning to do.

"Yo, Rashad?" Malik called out to the one he was more familiar with. They both looked back over their shoulders at him and paused for him to catch up.

Behind them, Junior stood on the front porch watching them, not anxious to make a move yet. He wanted to hang back just enough to observe the situation and be there fast enough when he needed him.

"One of y'all got a light?" Malik asked, producing the half blunt he still had in his possession.

It was Fonzo who gave him the lighter, all the while shivering in the cold outside. At fifteen, Fonzo was a stocky built kid with peach fuzz of a mustache growing over his top lip. The year he did in a juvenile bootcamp program had him in shape but surprisingly unruly for someone who did hard time.

"Where y'all headed?" Malik asked, handing back the lighter.

Fonzo shrugged and Rashad said they were going to go see if they could chill at Meat Rogers spot.

"Y'all can come to my crib. I got the new PS4 and all kinds of games we can play and smoke too. "Malik offered without a hint of maliciousness.

Both Fonzo and Rashad looked at each other.

"We're down with that," said Rashad.

"Let's go."

Leading the way to his house, Malik glanced over his shoulder to see Junior stalking behind them with his black hoodie pulled tight over his head. Malik was passing the blunt between the three of them as they trekked on.

"Um, M-Money? You know Murda-K, don't you?" Rashad asked as he hit the blunt twice and passed it to Fonzo.

You know damn well that's my uncle, thought Malik with a look of cautiousness on his face. What was Rashad trying to pull here? Was he also down with Fonzo going against his uncle? So many questions filled Malik's head at that moment, but Malik had to will himself to remain humble.

"He's a street legend," said Malik. "I respect niggaz like Murda-K. It's gangstaz like him that'll live forever, man."

"Not after what's he got coming." Fonzo passed the blunt in turn.

"What do you mean by that, Fonzo?" He asked.

Fonzo said, "I heard the stories, and I'm not impressed. Murda-K is old news. He's washed up now."

"Once a gangsta, always a gangsta, Fonzo."

Rashad met Malik's gaze and what he saw in his eyes was enough fire to start a furnace.

Five minutes later, they made it around to Malik's house and went inside. There Malik hooked up the PlayStation 4 in the front room where he let both guys play first. He watched them battle it out on Grand Theft Auto for about three minutes before excusing himself.

Quickly, Malik entered his mother's bedroom where she kept her gun in the nightstand drawer. He had taken the gun on several occasions when he expected trouble amiss during his past street dealings. Having shot the gun before he was no longer uncomfortable with the vociferous sound it made or the kickback it pronounced. He retrieved his mother's gun and shoved its loaded clip inside.

The .380 automatic he had used a T-shirt in his room to wipe it clean of any prints. He'd watched TV many times and knew the important methods of corrupting DNA.

About twenty minutes later, he announced that he was about to spark up another blunt, but they had to smoke it out back. They smoked another blunt, he reentered the house through the backdoor during the last rotation. He told them to come back in when they were done smoking on the back porch.

Malik's adrenaline was pumping strong, his heart racing, but he was dedicated to his mission.

Gun at his side ready for his opportunity to perform, Malik hoped Fonzo walked through the door first.

With the backdoor opening a moment later, Malik lifted the gun and aimed it directly at Fonzo's chest the moment he stepped over the threshold. He had been looking back at

Rashad, but when he turned to face Malik and saw the gun, Fonzo froze instantly.

"What're you doing, M-Money?" Fonzo demanded.

"What my uncle shoulda did to you that night years ago," said Malik. Then before Fonzo could respond, he shot him dead center of his chest forcing him back through the door against Rashad. When Fonzo was shoved forward by Rashad pushing him away, another slug punched him in the stomach and then he crumpled to the floor. Dead.

What Malik did next was something straight out of a murder mystery novel. He planted the .380 automatic pistol in Fonzo's hand with his finger on the trigger. Then, he made Rashad kick the backdoor in to make it a forced entry. Then, he forced Rashad under gun point to listen to what he said and follow the instructions given. Because if he didn't he was going to see that his Uncle Murda-K murdered his whole entire family. Hearing this, Rashad was willing to do anything Malik told him to do.

Malik was scared as fuck… But he'd be damned if he showed it, or he would never be able to forgive himself.

***

Zamon was sitting upright in his wheelchair as he entered the sports bar that afternoon. He was there to meet a very important man who could give him what he desired.

"Hey, Professor. What can I do for you, buddy?" The bartender acknowledged Zamon upon his entrance.

"I'm here meeting a very important associate of mine, Robbie. But you could fix my usual, no ice. It's cold enough outside as it is."

Zamon was happy to be inside. Warmth.

"Tell me about it. Go get yourself settled and I'll have Nicky bring over your drink," said Robyn Alexander-Chevez, one of Zamon's favorite people in the world. Ever since he could remember he'd been coming to the sports bar, and never once had she had to take his car keys away from him because he'd drunk too much to drive.

Robbie was more a friend than a bartender. She was always there to lend him an understanding ear.

Turning toward the sitting area of the bar, Zamon scanned the room for his man. Moments later, a long haired white guy in a brown leather jacket and cap lifted an arm to get his attention. He was sitting at a table in the far corner of the bar near the pool tables nursing a drink of his own. Zamon wheeled his chair over to the table with a purpose.

"Todd Hauptman?" Zamon offered the man his hand.

"That's me. Can I get you a drink?"

"I have one already coming." Zamon looked up just as top-heavy Nicky Wyatt approached with his gin and tonic. "Thank you, Nicky." He smiled up at her.

"Anytime, professor." Nicky went on her way.

"I guess you're a regular here, eh?"

"Something like that. I tip good and they treat me like one of their own. But thanks for coming, Todd. I was having second thoughts about this situation, but the more I prolong it the less sleep I get worrying about it."

"I understand," said Todd, his long dark hair tied.

"Sure you do. You get people like me all the time to pay you to do what you're the best at doing."

"I don't know about being the best, but I'm very good at what I do, man. It provides for my family and my sick mother. So whatever it is that you want I will be sure to give it my best to bring you the results you desire."

"Thank you."

"Now who is it that you want me to find?"

Zamon paused for a long moment before answering. "My wife," he said desperately. "I believe she's being unfaithful and I wanna know everything you could give me."

And that's what was going on. Zamon contacted a private detective to prove what his wife has been up to lately. He was worrying himself to death about it, and Melody's latest behavior wasn't making it easy for him.

Zamon was pulling a real sucker move, but what other choice did he have? He'd tried everything he could ever imagine to save his marriage but nothing worked. Now he was being forced to do something he'd never thought he would do. It was sickening to the stomach. It was desperation.

But at least he would know the truth to find closure.

Chapter 22

That afternoon Trenika wheeled her car into the driveway. Aryanna was out on the front lawn, practicing her moves with a soccer ball while Donecia and little Kahlil watched from the porch steps of the house.

"Hey, mommy." Aryanna was tall and lean for her age.

"Hey, baby girl. What'cha doing?"

"Watch and learn, old woman." said Aryanna.

"Old woman?" Trenika halted, offended by her daughter's words of expression. "Whatever string bean!" She retorted.

Aryanna maneuvered the ball across the yard. When she was only a few feet away from Trenika, she kicked the ball hard, straight into the center of Kahlil's old, overturned baby's crib. "That's a score, mommy!" She shouted, raising her arms over her head in a sign of victory.

Kahlil clapped his hands from the porch steps while Donecia proceeded to record the performance with her cell phone.

"That's easy to do without any pressure being applied."

She looked up at her mother, tucking a long black curl of hair behind an ear. "What?"

"Let's see can you do it with me guarding the goal." Trenika called for Kahlil to come retrieve her purse and coat. Kahlil was eager to oblige as he gave Aryanna that look that spoke volumes where he understood the challenge.

"Alright, mommy." Aryanna was game. She retrieved the ball and carried it back to the far side of the yard.

136

Trenika cracked her knuckles and assumed a challenging stance in front of the goal. "Whenever you're ready, baby girl."

Instead of taking a direct route as she had before, Aryanna weaved her way across the yard, adroitly maneuvering the soccer ball with impressive movements. Trenika remained standing before the makeshift *goal*, but Aryanna pulled her off center with a clever footwork dance pattern, and before Trenika could recover she kicked the ball into the baby crib *goal*.

"Yay!" Kahlil jumped up and down in an excited victory.

"Who said Ary don't got game!" Aryanna replied.

Baring her teeth, Trenika lunged forward, tackling her, and following Aryanna down into the grass.

"Flag on the play! Foul!" Baby girl cried out as Kahlil hurried over and dived onto them both.

Trenika wrestled with her daughter on the cold ground. But she astounded her by rolling to her side and putting Trenika in a leg and arm-bar technique position that left Trenika totally useless. Trenika tapped out and Aryanna scrambled back up to her feet quickly. She sat up, panting. "Where did you learn to do that, baby girl?"

Aryanna shot a sly glance over at Donecia. "It's nothing but a defense tactic, mommy."

With the little four-year-old strength that he could muster, Kahlil helped pull his mother up to her feet.

"So, this is what Donecia teaching you when I'm not around?" Said Trenika

"I can explain!" Donecia interjected.

"No. You don't have to take up for me, Donecia. I gotta do this my way," said Aryanna.

But before anyone else could respond, Naja's car pulled up in the driveway behind Trenika's. Also occupying the car with Naja were two more women, both of them equally beautiful and sexy as Naja were. Trenika invited them all into her home and proceeded to fix everybody cups of her favorite hot chocolate to warm them up.

After seeing Matthew and going back to the gallery to finish up a few things, Trenika decided to go home for the day. Before leaving the gallery she phoned Naja and requested that she meet her at the house by 3:00 p.m.. Naja was right on time. She was always prompt about her business. When everybody was served their drinks, Trenika summoned her friend to the home study which was her husband's office. "Have a seat, Naja."

"This sounds serious," said Naja.

"It is," Trenika assured her. "Do you know who Matthew Wu is?" She asked, sitting across from Kaedon's cousin before the desk.

"The same Matthew Wu that you had lunch with today at Outback Steakhouse? Yes. I know exactly who he is and why he's here in Atlanta," said Naja.

"Why?" Trenika didn't let on that she was baffled.

"To intervene in what I was paid to do. And I believe he is also responsible for Miami Shane's disappearance. So if you've called me here to prevent me from executing my side of the deal with that evil old bitch because he convinced you that I shouldn't, then you got another thing coming, cuz. Because if I have to kill him to get to Miami Shane then Matthew Wu is a dead muthafucker, cuz."

"Are you done?" Trenika gave her that testy look.

"A long way from it," Naja spoke.

"Drink your hot chocolate. Now." Trenika leaned forward in her seat. "You're right, Naja. He does want you to spare the life of Miami Shane."

"Not gonna happen."

"Not even for a million dollars to kill Vivian Wu?" Trenika asked and Naja damned near choked from her drink.

"What?" She said, wiping her mouth. "What did you say?"

"A million dollars, Naja."

A million dollars? Mulled Naja in silent anxiety. For that type of money she would kill the President of the United States.

Trenika read the answer in Naja's eyes without her even saying it out loud. She would do it. No doubt. Which meant Vivian Wu was a dead old bitch.

Ciera was sitting at the kitchen table with old man Jake and her new boyfriend Jerrod, her sister from another mother, Takeya, and Pam Bunion from Havana. When Kaedon entered the house and saw all of them present, he didn't care to speak with either of them except to know where his nephew was.

"He's in his room," said Jerrod, standing up to greet Kaedon with a handshake.

Not today. Kaedon wanted to see Malik, not socialize with anybody, not even with Tyquan, who was in the living room looking dejected and scared.

Kaedon marched down the hall straight for Malik's bedroom. He was about forty minutes away when he got the call from his sister about what Malik had done. Kaedon made it there in twenty-something minutes with the way he floored his truck all the way there. He tested the door and found it locked.

"Open the door, Malik." he ordered.

Seconds passed before the sound of the door being unlocked was heard and Kaedon opened the door.

Malik was inside his room listening to 102.3 Jamz playing from his old stereo sound system in an attempt to drown out the voices outside his bedroom door. Kaedon went over to the stereo and lowered the volume some, not outright cutting it completely off.

"Okay, Malik." Kaedon turned toward Malik sitting on the edge of his bed. "What happened?"

"I did it for you," Malik replied humbly.

"For me?"

He nodded.

"Explain that to me, nephew?" Kaedon saw something in his demeanor that looked very familiar to him that it almost made him scared for his nephew.

With a deep breath, Malik began his elaboration on what went down earlier today.

As he listened Kaedon had to take a seat himself, because what he was being told was seriously troubling. Here it was, his almost thirteen-year-old nephew having just premeditatedly murdered another kid in honor of his name. Kaedon didn't know whether to be honored or cry.

But there was something it did do, which made Kaedon go back to that night so many years ago. A lot of heat was sure to come down with what happened today. Kaedon had to also make sure Malik's name is secured too, because what he did was out of loyalty.

"Did you cover all your tracks, Malik?"

"I did everything I knew you would do, Unc." Malik then went on to say how he wiped down the game controllers clean and everywhere in the house that Rashad and Fonzo may have touched.

"You did good, little nigga. You really did."

"I did?" Malik took his uncle's praise to the chest and when Kaedon stood up to show him some love. It was all he could do not to start crying. This was the moment he had always dreamed of.

He dreamt of his uncle's acceptance and his honoring him for his gangsta.

"Mama is pissed at me," he said.

"Don't worry about it," Kaedon reassured him. "I'll take care of your mama." He told Malik.

And so the nightmares will begin, thought Kaedon. He remembered when Trenika had killed Romell five years ago and how every night after that she woke up screaming from the nightmares. He himself had experienced his share of nightmares after his first kill. They eventually went away with time, but he knew for a fact Malik would have them.

Chapter 23

With the rise of the sun the following morning, came the surprising news of the horrific murders of LaShonda Hughs and her nine-year-old son Draydon. There was also a third murder at the same residence, where twenty-nine-year-old Trent Conyers was found shot to death on the front porch. There was a suspect, and he was Brandon Wells Junior aka Junior, whom a witness claimed they spotted him leaving the house after the crime took place.

While eating bowls of Lucky Charms cereal with his nephews, Kaedon and Malik met each other's gaze at the table. They both knew what it meant in regard to the murders. That Junior had gone out his way to do what he thought was best in Malik's favor.

Years ago, Alonzo Dennis brought LaShonda up from the Florida Keys after she escaped Haiti with her family. Her parents died trying to save her and her brother Emmanuel, who was now serving life in prison for killing a tourist down in Miami to help provide for her. Lonzo gave LaShonda a life she never thought she deserved to have. All her family back in Haiti has written her off as dead. She only had friends and associates whom she loved and respected dearly. But no one would intervene in her honor, she had nobody who was willing to die avenging her death.

Not even Lonzo's family was going to risk the lives of what little family they had left.

Broken hearts happened when she and her family died, but no one wanted to defend their honor.

"When will all this senseless killing stop!" Ciera said and threw her dishes into the kitchen sink while breaking a bowl in the process. "Shit!"

"Cee Cee..." Kaedon set his spoon down and stood up.

"I don't wanna hear it, Kaedon. I can't do this shit anymore!" She snapped at him. "My son is a killer. My brotha is a killer... killers all around me! I can't do this. We can't stay here any longer, it's not safe. I'm putting in my two-week notice at the job and I'm gettin' the fuck outta Quincy. Fuck this place and everything it ever stood for," she cried.

Ciera stomped out of the kitchen and headed down the hall to her bedroom.

"Where will we go, Uncle Kaedon?" Tyquan asked.

"She's just upset, Ty. Don't sweat it. Your mama ain't leaving Quincy. She loves this country shit," Kaedon replied but not even he believed what he had just said to his nephew.

"She's not bullshittin'," said Malik.

Kaedon looked over at him and said, "She's scared, y'all. You mama is just worried sick about us. But you know what we have to do? We have to protect her and keep her safe and happy."

"I know what'll make her happy," said Tyquan.

"What, nephew?"

Tyquan said, "A vacation. Let's get her away from here for a while and take her to Busch Gardens or somewhere where there's fun. Mama would like that, huh?"

"And you'll just love it, Ty."

"Sounds like a plan," Kaedon nodded. "When I'm done here we're gonna do just that. I haven't been to Busch Gardens in years... I used to love roller coasters! Yeah. It's what all of us need. Good thinking, Ty guy!" He said and extended his fist over to his nephew for some dap.

Tyquan was pleased with himself.

After he was done with his breakfast, Kaedon nodded his head toward the front with Malik. He and Malik stood out on the front porch, watching as neighbors climbed into their cars in their winter gear.

"Give me your word you won't go out there lookin' for your partna," said Kaedon.

"I know where he's at, Unc. I don't need to look." Malik told him nonchalantly.

"Did you know about those murders too?"

"No."

Kaedon gave him a stern look.

"I didn't know," Malik insisted evenly. "Or else I woulda went with him to do it," he said.

"It's a good thang you didn't. But stay outta sight for now, Malik. It's too hot for you right now. The streets is watching. Especially now with me here they're really gonna be talkin' for sure. It won't surprise me if they're even suspecting me to have something to do with those murders. However, I need you to lay low and wait on my further instructions. Can you do that for me?"

"I can do it," said Malik, shivering in the cold.

"You gon' lay low?"

Malik nodded.

"Put that on King Von." Kaedon knew how to get Malik to keep his word. The little nigga was crazy over the now deceased rapper King Von. He'd even busted another kid's lip at the neighborhood park for dissing the rapper.

"On Von," Malik replied. "My word."

***

Jourdan pulled the car up to the curb out before the house and honked the horn. A minute later, Trenika and the kids exited the house for the car.

"I am so not with this cold," Trenika warmed her hands in front of the heater vents before her.

143

"Girl, this is nothing. Try the cold up in Chicago and you'll look at this weather like it's springtime compared to it. There's no cold like Chicago cold, honey." Jourdan can say that she was born and raised in Chicago. But going back home was the last thing she wanted; it was better to just forget about it.

"I like the cold weather," said Aryanna from the backseat next to her little brother.

"Baby girl got thick skin," Jourdan remarked.

They were on their way to drop the children off on Lisa and her husband Byron, and their three-year-old son Jabari Deshay. Lisa was taking them all out to the mall and a movie, while Trenika went to go get setup for her big event today.

After dropping the kids off it was then that Trenika finally let out a troubling sigh.

"You first or should I go?" Said Jourdan, enroute to the gallery to go help her friend out. Jourdan owned her own catering company, and it was her company that was responsible for the food and the champagne that was going to be floating around the building. Her company was in high demand and people loved her services.

"You go first," said Trenika. "I still don't even know where to begin in all this."

"Just start from the beginning of your troubles."

"I wished it was that easy."

Jourdan reached over and rubbed her friend's back. "Well. I'm pregnant again," she said.

Trenika gasped and looked at her in disbelief. "Really?"

"Yep. At forty-six years old. I've known for about a week now; I just came to grips with what it all means. And you know I don't believe in abortions, Tee."

"How far along are you, Jourdan?"

"Five and a half weeks."

Trenika didn't know how to take such news. She didn't know anyone who brought a child into this world while still in their forties. And here it was Jourdan was four years from fifty and nearly six weeks pregnant. *That could be a serious health hazard for her and the child,* thought Trenika.

"I know what you're thinking, Tee," said Jourdan

"My concern is natural, Jourdan. Are you sure this is what you really wanna do?"

"Let's just call it my early retirement gift to the world. God would not allow this to happen if it wasn't destined."

"Does Al know?"

"Not yet. I wanted to tell my sister first. Now. What is ailing you already on this fine beautiful day?"

Trenika still couldn't shake the fact that Jourdan was pregnant. What was even so amazing about it was Jourdan being happy about it and not scared to death over it. Because she could very much lose her baby to still born or even jeopardize her own life in the process. There were so many dangers with being forty-six and pregnant with a child.

Trenika shook her head and hoped to God that her friend was safe to proceed with it.

"Kae lied to me last night – yesterday rather," said Trenika.

"About what, Tee?"

"Why he needed to go back home to Quincy for a few days," said Trenika. "He would later say he lied to protect me."

Jourdan heard the hurt in Trenika's voice.

"To protect you from what?"

"The mission."

"What mission, Trenika?"

"To kill again," Trenika cried and folded her arms across her chest. "I can't go through this again, Jourdan. I have my children's futures to protect. They could never be safe with him out there being a gangsta. He promised me that it was all over. But it's not over, Jourdan. It's not gonna be over till my dreams finally come true."

"And what dreams are these exactly?"

A deep emotion burned in Trenika's chest. "The ones where some faceless enemy comes for us for something Kaedon's done and make us watch as they kill him. Then, there's the one where Ary is taken and killed. And then me," she said softly and closed her eyes. "I can't even put it into words what was done to me in these dreams. And last night when I woke up from one of those dreams, Kaedon wasn't there to assure me everything would be okay."

"That's deep, girlfriend," Jourdan whispered.

"LuLu was there to bring me the comfort I needed," said Trenika "A muthafuckin' dog! An animal. While he's out there being no different from the monster Romell was."

"Don't go there, Tee."

"I've went there, Jourdan. Too many times. I'm fed up. And before I allow his bullshit to come back and haunt us, I will kill Kaedon my damn self." Trenika was dead serious and no doubt capable of doing it.

When a woman's fed up… There ain't nothing you could do about it. Kaedon had to get his shit together. Or get left behind.

Chapter 24

The information that Naja had provided was accurate and Kaedon couldn't believe his luck at how easily a target Lenny Baker was making himself.

Lenny had relocated to Tallahassee, Florida which was only just a few miles from Quincy. When the money got longer and the game got deeper, relocating to a more secure spot was a necessity. He lived in a gated community that housed the likes of a judge, politicians, some lawyers and even the chief of police, which meant heavy security and around the clock guarding. He was living right under the noses of the very people who opposed his way of life.

That's not to mention the high-rise penthouse Lenny owned now as well. He didn't believe in creating a family of his own for fear of jeopardizing their lives with his risky position. He never went without a pocketful of condoms. A womanizer he was, but never the type to fall in love. It was too dangerous, and love made a man weak.

Lenny had a successful hand in a few businesses too, creating opportunities for his community to find work. That's one of the good things he had going on beside dishonor and being the snake that he was. All snakes deserved to die.

Kaedon hadn't had to search for too long to locate that snake which was Lenny Baker. He had caught him in the nick of time pushing his Porsche Cayenne Bi-Turbo SUV through traffic along South Monroe Street. Lenny was making his rounds and Kaedon followed him in an old Dodge Neon like a prowling wolf on the scent of a wounded doe.

Riding alongside of him was his most trusted goon by the name of Thirsty, one whom the streets between the two counties was always weary of. Thirsty was a stone-cold killer that has escaped death numerous times. But today he was about to get his ticket punched out.

Today the streets would both mourn and rejoice their deaths. There was no escaping the inevitable.

Twenty-three minutes of watching Lenny make his rounds throughout the city, he finally made the mistake of getting out of the truck at this certain location. That location was the Player's Choice Barbershop spot that he owned. Lenny was said to be a great barber himself, having come up cutting hair in the hood to keep money in his pockets. Now, he owned a few Player's Choice Barbershops which were there in Tallahassee, down in Quincy, and even down in St. Pete where his cousin PayPay lived and managed. This was one Lenny's regular spot to frequent, for he was strict about keeping his haircut sharp. He had some of the best barbers in business.

Speaking of which, Kaedon was cutting to the chase and moving into position for execution. He decided on a location about three hundred yards away tucked in a side pocket space of a local tattoo shop's parking lot. From this vantage point Kaedon is positioned on the side of the barber shop where he would have a clear shot of Lenny's left temple.

Here, Kaedon retrieved the sniper's rifle with the scope from the floor in the back and shifted in his shooting position and waited for that cruel moment to execute.

Once Lenny was dead, it was on to Mike-Mike and his brother Rico. Everybody involved had to get dealt with accordingly. They were the major players in the game and taking them all out would put a cease to their whole existence.

Kaedon's grandfather and grandmother were both avid hunters. Growing up sniping off eight-point bucks and boar hogs and rabbits were fun for him back when he was ten. Then, when his grandfather died it led to his grandmother's depression, and their hunting expeditions had come to a halt. Well, at least hunting animals were, because several years ahead Kaedon took to hunting humans. So his way with a rifle was not lost on him, for Kaedon would always know how to handle such weapons.

He was a true marksman by trade.

So when Lenny finally emerged from the barber shop an hour later sporting a fresh cut, Kaedon sighted through the scope of the rifle and zeroed in on the mark's hairline. A deep breath. Relax. And squeeze the trigger. From three hundred yards away, the 17-grain bullet smashed into the side of Lenny's head and splattered the whole front of the building with his brains. Instinctively, Thirsty paused then reached for his sidearm, and the second bullet punched him right through his left eye socket dropping him dead.

"Easy as pumpkin pie," muttered Kaedon.

And then he got ghost.

Ten minutes later while cruising down Orange Avenue with the double murder put at the back of his mind, Kaedon received a phone call from his cousin Naja.

"What's up, cuz?"

Naja said, "One of my girls, Yvonne, will be giving you a call in a minute."

"Giving me a call for what?" He asked.

"The next location." she told him.

"Where to?"

"Where you'll find both little cubs in the same spot already prepared for the slaughter. Don't ask questions. I love you, cuz. I'll see you when you get back home," Naja replied. She was indicating that she knew the whereabouts of Mike-Mike and Rico and was already preparing their death certificates.

All Kaedon could do was shake his head. His cousin was truly a gangstress for real, and with a team of thorough bitches who'll kill for her on sight.

This really needed to be the end of his problems. Kaedon was tired of going through the same ol' shit.

***

Ciera got Tyquan and left the house for old man Jake's to take him out to the flea market in Tallahassee. It was one of Jake's favorite places to go on Saturdays. He and his wife Sylvia used to go there every weekend.

Malik was left at home to do as his uncle said. At first Ciera didn't want to leave him, but knew babying him would only frustrate Malik. Late last night he woke her up out of a fitful sleep and told her the truth about why he killed Fonzo. She cried on his shoulder and told him how scared she was of losing her family.

Everything appeared to be falling to pieces, but Malik assured her that everything would be okay. He was the black sheep. He was their protector.

"They gone?" Junior peeped his head out of Malik's bedroom and said.

"Yeah. They won't be back for a few hours at the flea market. Jake can't be on his feet for long periods of time. You want something to eat, my nigga?"

"Hell yeah!"

Sometime around three in the morning, Junior came knocking on Malik's bedroom window. It was then that he told Malik all about what he did to the rest of Fonzo's family. He wasn't taking any chances of LaShonda striking out against Malik or his family to avenge her son's death.

The two road dawgs entered the kitchen where Junior fixed himself a bowl of cereal.

"I heard what mama Cee said this morning too," said Junior, having chosen to eat Fruit Loops instead. "You really think she'll get ghost from here?" He asked.

"I don't know, Junior."

"I think y'all should leave for a while, brah. It ain't nothing here but bad memories and endless drama. I don't want to see you get hurt, my nigga. Or your family. Encourage her to finally get outta the hood. Niggaz like us don't last long here," said Junior. "I was thinking about it myself."

"You gettin' outta the hood? Yeah right."

"That's what I was saving up for, M-Money. I was just waiting on mama to get out of jail and move her away from this place. This ain't living, my nigga."

"And take Leah with you?" Malik smirked.

He nodded.

Although she was young, Leah was a real bitch who understood him like no other. She comes from a good breed of family; both of her parents were successful business owners. Leah just liked what she liked and being the girlfriend of a street nigga was totally against their beliefs.

Junior seemed to have it all figured out.

"But with this murder shit hanging in the air," Malik begin as he opened the fridge and took out a pack of grapes. "You'll only be on the run or looking over your shoulder, Junior."

"I got a plan," said Junior.

"I need to find out who that witness is."

A hand slapped against the table splashing milk from the bowl of cereal. "Stop that shit, dawg. I'm going through it already as it is for pushing you to handle that nigga Fonzo. I shoulda just did it myself. But you did what you had to do, and your show is over. Stay outta this shit, brah. Stick to hustling and gettin' to that bag. I'm the soulja. That's my position between us. Leave all that murder shit to me. When I say I got a plan I mean that, M-Money. You my lil' brah

151

and I want what's best for you, but you have to focus on what matters the most."

"It's too late for that, Junior," said Malik.

Junior just stared angrily at him.

"I got blood on my hands now, brah. You're right, hustling is what I do, but you're not always gonna be there to watch my back. I have to prove my murder game too!"

"I'll always be there, Malik," he vowed.

Malik didn't question him on that and decided to just let the matter drop.

"We all we got, my nigga," Junior told him.

Malik nodded. "We all we got."

But he still was going to do whatever he had to do to survive in life. And if that meant killing niggas in the process then that's what he will do.

Case closed.

Chapter 25

"Another glass of champagne, Mrs. Smith?" Said the uniformed waiter holding a silver tray balancing a bucket of chilled bubbly inside. Her smile was bright and colorful.

Trenika looked up from where she was standing amongst her group of guests. "No, thank you," she said.

The waitress then refilled two more glasses among the group and hurried off to keep other drinks freshened.

Having changed earlier into a cream-colored Jonathan Simkhai silk dress and heels with a fancy fox fur coat draped over her shapely frame, Trenika was the hostess but also the center of attention. She was the beautiful woman of the hour that brought out four hundred and twenty guests to marvel over her pieces and meet and greet one another. Even the Mayor of Tallahassee had come out and complimented her success.

Trenika couldn't keep the smile from her face. She was really in her element today.

The stresses of what lied beyond those gallery doors was no longer existent to her. Trenika was engulfed with excitement and basking in the glow of being admired for her hard work and dedication. She had brought together all styles and life of the art society.

And boy did she know how to work the room full of artistic guests. Trenika had a knack for such things. People took to her like a moth to a flame. She was just so fascinating to be around. Cultivating to be exact.

Then, suddenly an arm hooked through hers and when Trenika looked to see who it was, her eyes bulged in unexpected surprise at seeing Aryanna at her side. In her hand was a flute of something orange, to which Trenika knew was her daughter's favorite soda. But what astounded Trenika even more was the also cream colored Halston gown Aryanna was wearing with the brownish hue Laligne sweater she had on to complement her fashion. A brilliant smile lit up Aryanna's face when she saw Trenika blushing down at her.

"What are you doing here, Ary?"

Aryanna said, "I made Aunt Lisa bring me here because I knew we would rock the crowd together."

"Rock the crowd?" Said Trenika

"Watch and learn."

With that being said, Aryanna pulled her mother away from her guests and mingled through the gallery meeting and greeting the crowd. Within no time Aryanna's existence had recaptured that glow Trenika was already basking in and turned it into a full sunshine.

But the ultimate surprise came when Aryanna took the makeshift stage that was provided for the guest speakers and stood before the podium.

"Was this part of the program?" Olivia appeared next to Trenika in front of the stage.

Trenika was so stunned by her daughter's performance that she didn't notice all those she loved and cared for dearly was standing amongst her. "She's stealing my shine," she said.

"Not when you're shining together," Apryl replied, her glass of Champagne in hand.

"Ary is rocking the crowd just like she said."

"Hello everybody," Aryanna said into the microphone where which a handsome older gentleman had readjusted to her height level. "How is everybody doing today?"

Everybody in the room responded in unison as all eyes were on the beautiful ten-year-old.

"My mommy didn't expect this moment but I'm pretty sure she's loving it," Aryanna said as she received a minor pleasant response from the crowd. "My mommy always said that art reveals beauty in the smallest details of creation. It finds light in the darkest shadow. It's a guide and a teacher, reminding others that life is a miracle, something to be celebrated like today. Art has become my mommy's strength, and most times her weakness. She taught me that art tells deep truths about joy and pain, triumph and grief. I've seen my mommy paint the greatest pictures through her own tears. But when people see the finished work it makes them smile, or simply nod with admiration. That's why I believe art can be healing for anyone. Because through her darkness her art has brought the brightest light into the world. Thank you." She bowed.

And then came the round of applause from the whole room as Trenika couldn't help herself and let her tears run free with joyous love for her daughter.

"That was beautiful, baby girl," said Kaedon as he stepped forward to help Aryanna down from the stage.

"Kae…" Trenika swallowed hard as she turned a wild, tearful gaze at her husband. "You came?"

"I couldn't miss out on my wife's big day," said Kaedon, having made it there in time to capture the moment that would have made any parent proud.

Trenika hugged her man. "I love you so much, Kaedon. Thank you for coming," she cried.

"I wouldn't have missed it for the world. Our daughter is a wonderful speaker, huh?"

"She's the best."

He nodded. "And you too," Kaedon kissed her cheek. "You too."

***

That evening Naja was wearing a pair of black fitted jeans, high top Nike ACG shoes, and a smoke gray and black cotton twill varsity blazer. Naja was very coordinated with clothes, but tonight she was dressed to look the part. She was occupying the table booth in the back of a local Burger King restaurant eating a Whopper with fries. After sitting down she only had to wait about seven minutes before Vivian Wu entered the building with her trained dog in tow. Upon entering the fast food joint the Asian woman turned up her nose at the variety of smells. It was evident her expensive nose didn't approve with the scent of cheap Burger King food. She was a woman of quality tastes. A spoiled old bitch.

"Ranaja, honey. What is so important that you had to call me out to this... dump of an eatery?" Said Vivian Wu, climbing into the tight space of the table booth in front of Naja and her meal.

"You've never eaten at Burger King before?"

"Never," the Asian woman cringed with obvious distaste.

"How about you?" Naja looked up at the other woman who remained standing guard at her boss's side. She just stared coldly at Naja and not saying a word. "Well, you don't know what you're missing," she said.

"Get to the point of this meeting, will you?"

"Your grandson, Matthew."

Vivian stiffened. "What about Matthew?"

"He's here in Atlanta. And I believe he has taken Miami Shane underground somewhere."

This was bad news to the older woman. "You have any idea where he could have possibly taken him? I'm sure you know, Naja, given your remarkable resources. It's really the main reason why I chose you for this job. Can you find both of them and... you know the rest."

"That'll have to cost you," Naja said.

"Five hundred thousand. No exceptions. When can you get it done." asked Vivian Wu, leaning forward to speak in a hushed tone of voice.

Right then the restroom door opened behind Naja as two women made their exit.

The Asian woman sat upright in her seat as she watched both women proceed to walk past them. Then out of nowhere a six-inch blade was jabbed into the neck of Vivian's sidekick and another blade to the left kidney by both unexpected killers passing by.

"Your grandson sends his regards." Naja rose up to her feet as she watched the Asian boss get her throat slit from ear to ear. "You wasn't talking my language bitch." Naja didn't even wait up to witness the old woman take her last breath. She had faith in her bitches.

They were ruthless.

Chapter 26

A laugh was just at the tip of Kaedon's lips as he watched the video of Aryanna and Trenika soccer challenge from Donecia's phone. When he got to the point where the two ended up wrestling and seeing Trenika tap out he frowned.

"I know what that look means," said Lisa.

"What look?" Jourdan asked.

The living room that evening was filled with people as they all sat around talking and kicking it. Lisa and her family were there, little Sasha, Malik, whom Kaedon had brought home with him, and Pooh Baby and one of his female friends. Young Kahlil was going around the room sharing his bag of gummy bears with everybody.

It was a nice home gathering.

Donecia explained the Jujitsu defense technique that she had taught Aryanna. Her father had encouraged her and her brother to attend Karate classes since they were little. She stuck with her training in martial arts while Alex Junior decided on pursuing his love for basketball.

This Jourdan had clarified on where her children's decisions were concerned.

"When we all started making our own choices in life nothing stopped us from doing what we wanted to do," said Byron, a solid guy with a growing beer belly.

"You're right, brah." Agreed Kaedon. "But the lessons we learn before then are always instilled in us too. We might haven't turned out the way our parents imagined or prepared

158

for us to be. But their teachings we will always remember, because it's what led us to be who we are today."

"What do you consider yourself as, Kaedon?" Asked Cheryl, the friend whom Pooh Baby invited over with him. She was a unique looking mulatto chick with dark blue eyes.

"A gangsta," said Kaedon.

"A gangsta, really?" Cheryl replied in doubt.

He nodded.

For all those who knew Kaedon, they understood the meaning in which he referred to himself as.

Kaedon summed his whole life up for Cheryl in the matter of five minutes. But he went on to add that being a gangsta wasn't solely based on the negative aspect of things. He identified the morals and the integrity, and the principles the man lived by that makes a gangsta who he is.

"Being a gangsta taught me the values of love, honor, and responsibility," said Kaedon.

"Damn," said Donecia. "How can a person make being a gangsta sound so honorable?"

"Because it is," Trenika said as she sat upon the couch next to Kaedon with her feet resting in his lap.

The vibration of the cellphone against the glass tabletop in front of the couch stole Kaedon's attention. He reached for his phone and read the text message sent to him.

Turn to the news: said the text message.

Kaedon grabbed the remote control and turned the TV to the local news channel.

The news reporter: "… of an Asian mob organization was brutally murdered this evening inside a local Burger King restaurant. Resources say the deceased Asian crime boss was responsible for over fifty homicides that transpired throughout the U.S. since January 1st. According to the Atlanta Police Department, three women was seen fleeing the scene during the incident, but none has been yet identified. The investigation is still underway –" Trenika powered the TV off.

"And that is what that gangsta stuff gets you if you're not careful," said Jourdan.

Eyes slyly glanced in Kaedon's direction.

He got up and left the room for his study office and shut the door behind him.

The text message had come from Naja herself. Kaedon had no doubt in his mind that his cousin was one of those three women. But knowing Naja like he does, she had the situation under control. However, he couldn't help but worry and needed to hear her voice.

"Yes, cuz. I'm good. I've been outta town all day in Augusta with my wifey," Naja said the instant she answered her cousin's phone call.

Malik entered the office next as Kaedon stared at him in silent acknowledgment.

"How is the fam in Augusta?" Kaedon asked.

"Rich," she said.

He smirked. "They better be with the type of work they put in tending cattle," he said.

Naja laughed. "Them heifers are good money!"

"But you sure you're okay, cuz?" His tone dropped to that volume laden with genuine concern.

"Shut up with all that soft ass shit, cuz. I said I was good. Now," she replied. "Where is Malik?"

"He's right here." Kaedon looked up at his nephew.

Naja growled. "Put his badazz on the phone," she spat, madly.

***

The next several days for Malik were spent doing hard labor working at his uncle's truck yard, in the bar and lounge cleaning the place up, and even earning some learning skills working as a temporary trimmer for the landscaping company that Kaedon owned as well. Whatever his uncle was trying to accomplish by making him work so hard the way he did, Malik didn't complain and tackled his tasks without even questioning Kaedon's motives for slaving him.

Something in Malik motivated him to take his challenges to the chest and push through it.

By the fifth day of labor, Malik had come to understand what was being demanded of him. The values of responsibility were shaping up. Malik didn't consider this as a form of punishment for getting suspended from school – no punishment was even intended for that matter. But he did recognize quite a few opportunities he could use to his benefit. Malik had learned to embrace his hard labor for what it was. His cleverness was kicking in. He was plotting.

On the seventh day, which was the day of his thirteenth birthday, Malik didn't even think about home or celebrating his blessed day. He was strategizing a way to showcase his hustle game. There was something he dared to try and by doing this, he needed a team player. Somebody that he could trust beyond measure. The ultimate sidekick.

And what better partner in crime than his very own road dawg. When called, Junior came running like the true friend that he was.

Having reflected on their recent conversation about where one another stood in this game of life, Malik thought it was best to utilize their positions to the best of their abilities.

With his plan in motion, Malik knew without a shadow of doubt that the money would come pouring in.

By his second week there in Atlanta, with a few days left before he returned back to school, Malik began his new hustle with no one being the wiser with what he was doing. This hustle was done quietly and without drawing attention to himself or those in which he cared about. Not even Kaedon was hip to this new hustle, and it was being done right there in his face. Malik was smart and talented, but it was his devious trickery that was worth the risk of being discreet.

The night before leaving back for home, Trenika pulled him aside to speak with him privately. While everybody was entertaining themselves in the spacious kitchen making rice krispies treats, he was led to the den area.

"What's up, auntie?" He replied.

Trenika smiled shyly at the endearment of being called *auntie*. I hope you've learned your lesson being here with us. Kae had his own reasons for bringing you here, but what we shared while you were here was something special. You've always been an intelligent young man but learn to use that intelligence more wisely," she expressed.

"I am," Malik said humbly.

"I just bet you are, M-Money," she smirked and Malik gave her a surprised look. "Yeah, I know your little name. And I know you have plans by bringing more meaning to that name as well. Again, just make sure you do it wisely, because there's more than one way to skin a cat. The world has millions of different ways to make money and make your uncle proud of you. The street life doesn't always have to be your only source of demand. Think outside the box, baby boy."

"I understand, auntie. I know what to do now."

"And protect yourself and your family, okay."

He nodded. "Always."

"Now gimme some love," she opened out her arms to him and Malik hugged her.

Then, suddenly out of nowhere LuLu came over and roughed him up for a minute to separate them both.

"And yes," Trenika laughed. "She does get jealous, too."

Chapter 27

Months went by without further serious incident, though the smoke was still up in relevance to the Vivian Wu's assassination, and a few minor incidents with the cops harassing Malik about the Fonzo murder. They picked him up once while in a convenience store in an attempt to make him sweat. But Malik kept his cool and never gave the two cops the satisfaction of seeing him sweat. Other than that all was well with the home front. Malik continued his cigarette grind while Junior maintained their other silent hustle up in Atlanta along with Leah. He was still a man in question in the murders of Fonzo's family but there was no concrete evidence to actually convict him. Only a credible witness stood in the way and Junior claims he had a possible lead on just who that witness was.

Until then, the grind must go on.

Furthermore, the capture of Tyreek took place over in Texas where he had been staying below the radar living with a distant relative. Until his Molly habit got the best of him and he took to extorting college kids and sticking up Uber drivers. He was sleeping one evening during a hot June day on the back patio when he was awakened surrounded by cops with their guns drawn on him. After they were done with him in Texas, he would be extradited back to Quincy to face the fire there. The nigga was so stupid.

Aryanna had had her first period during a pool party in her backyard amongst friends and family. Never in her life had she been so embarrassed and scared. She rushed to her mother thinking she was having a baby, but Trenika, along with all the other women present, convinced her that she wasn't having a baby but experiencing her first womanly cycle.

That was a shame baby girl would never forget.

However, she did manage to get promoted to the sixth grade and being in middle school really shaped her essence. Not only was she on the girl's soccer team but in the school's band too, playing the clarinet and was becoming damn good at it too. Aryanna went from being the fresh faced sixth grader who became prey to the older girls, to getting suspended for beating up two seventh graders at the same time, to becoming the respected, feared young freshman. Before long it didn't take a rocket scientist to see that baby girl was not the one to be crossed.

By the time little Kahlil was in the second grade and playing junior league football, Aryanna was gradually becoming popular and interested in boys.

It was after Aryanna's fourteenth birthday did Kaedon noticed her change in clothing and her wearing more revealing attire. It was a fear of its own seeing how much his baby girl has grown into a beautiful young woman that all the boys wanted a piece of. Aryanna pretended boys didn't interest her like they did all her friends, but she had no qualms about dressing so suggestively pretentious and using boys' weaknesses against them.

Of course, it was that time that her and Kaedon had that talk about how boys think. To him, Aryanna made it a point of convincing him that what was most important to her was school and her dreams of going to Clark Atlanta. She wanted to prove herself responsible and even though she was interested in boys, she knew to respect herself and exercise her dignity by being steadfast in keeping her innocence intact.

Four years had flown by since Kaedon remembered when she was just a ten-year-old still peeing the bed and so innocent it made you cry. But here she was now, a teenager and developing into a model young lady with big dreams.

Trenika, who was seeing the first signs of gray in her hair, had been the link to keep her family strong. There were times when she wanted to call it quits due to Kaedon's endless street affairs, but her love for him kept her immovable. Especially after old man Jake died at eighty-two and Kaedon took his anger out on those he may have considered his foes. He had killed two people during his mourning period, one of which had been brought to their front door. The guy whom he had been suspected of killing, was the cousin of Malik's father.

Harrold Mitchell had come back to county on appeal for his case and had demanded to see Malik. Malik went to visit him in the county a few times just out of curiosity. But when Malik – then sixteen – told Harrold what it was and how he wasn't feeling the daddy-son thing he was trying to force upon him, Malik left and never came back. Then Harrold sent his so-called goon of a cousin to the house to confront Malik about his behavior. But the worst thing he could have ever done was disrespect Ciera. Two days afterwards, the nigga was found beaten to death with a blunt object in his apartment downtown. For about a week and some change two detectives from the Homicide Dept. of the QPD and one from the Atlanta PD made it their business to hound Kaedon at every corner. They came to the house looking for him several times before Trenika kicked him out and told him that his foolishness was bringing harm to their family.

That's when Tazzy and Aunt Amy came down for a visit and talked some sense into Trenika. By then, Kaedon had been gone a whole week, but never too far from home to keep a close eye on his family.

During that period, Kaedon had succumbed to the lure of the harassing investigating officers and with the powerful assistance of his faithful lawyer, Veronica Dunn, they left the police station laughing their asses off. The following day, Trenika called her husband home and there has been no trouble in paradise since. Kaedon was back to the humbled, loving, sweet gangsta that he's always been since the first moment they met.

Speaking of which, Kaedon was there with his twin brother when Zamon filed for divorce. Melody indeed had been committing adultery against Zamon by sleeping with his colleague at the college. Her disloyalty had crushed Zamon so much that he contemplated taking his own life. It had gotten so bad that Zamon fired his personal caregiver, drowned his pain in alcohol to the point it landed him in the intensive care unit, and sliced his wrists. Zamon had to be admitted to a mental health hospital where he underwent treatment for his mental disability. Kaedon learned of this when it was too late and went to go rescue his beloved brother. He took him home with him and became his caregiver until he got Zamon back to where he could perform on his own independence.

When Kaedon thought his life couldn't get any more complicated than it was already, Zamon had taken him through hell. He lived with his brother for a full year until he himself demanded to leave because Kaedon had totally abducted him.

Trenika cried when she watched him go.

So far Zamon has been doing good on his own. But he has been fighting tooth and nail to share custody of his son, Zion. Because he had taken everything from her, Melody was making it hard for him. Though the court saw it in his favor to have visitation privileges with his now nine-year-old son.

All the lives revolving around Kaedon were too serious to take for granted.

Naja was enjoying her new riches and queen status. She eventually married her longtime partner, Cookie Jones, and was living it up out in Upstate New York. Cookie wanted to go back to where she came from in Memphis, so Naja bought her a nice townhouse there. There wasn't nothing she wouldn't do for her wife and Naja gave her the world.

And so had Lance to his woman Quanda, who he hadn't married yet, but instead purchased her dream home out in Hollywood, California. Thanks to Naja being his personal connect now, his hustle had rewarded him more money than he could ever dream of. Killing the Asian grandmother rewarded Naja a million dollars, and a generous drug connect in Matthew Wu that Lance was utilizing for all it was worth.

Life was good in the streets for Lance and Naja, while Malik was slowly climbing the ranks with his position in the streets. And that's where the story of their lives proceeded with what was to happen next.

***

"Fuck…!" Kaedon gagged, convulsed, and let another spew of vomit splashing into the commode as he hugged its chrome for dear life. He was sweating profusely; his chest cavity tighten as he heaved and threw up his guts.

Trenika came rushing into the bathroom at 3:19 a.m. with a cold damp rag to place against his forehead as she rubbed her husband's back soothingly. "Let it out, baby. Let it out."

This was the second night in a row Kaedon has woken up in cold sweats and fighting to keep from choking on his throw-up. At first Trenika chalked it up as something Kaedon had probably eaten, but now she was worried of it being something entirely.

When Kaedon was done puking all over the place, Trenika reached up and flushed the toilet. He then climbed to his feet and proceeded to brush his teeth.

While Kaedon went to go lay back down, Trenika spent the next ten minutes cleaning up the bathroom. When she finally emerged she found her husband in bed laying on his side staring into the darkness. She joined him back in bed beneath the silk sheets and nestled up behind Kaedon in the spooning position. She rested her head against his back and curled her arm around him.

"I think it's happening, bae," he sighed.

Trenika felt her heart squeeze with emotion as the weight of his words began to settle upon her.

"I've began noticing my weight droppin' too," he spoke up again. "No matter how much I eat it still drops but gradually. Now the night sweats and the vomiting. It's happening. It took a while but it's happening," he cried. "I'm dying."

"No no no no. Don't say that. We will go see the doctor tomorrow," she told him.

"I know that's what it is, Trenika." Kaedon sat up in bed with his back against her. "I knew the risks before I did it. But I did it because I love you, not anythang else. I have H.I.V. now and that's what it is," he said before getting up and walking out of the room.

"Please God..." cried Trenika as she lay there thinking about her situation. She too knew that this moment would come, but it scared her just thinking about it. She knew a person could have H.I.V. but still go up to ten years without being detected. She was just a carrier of the virus; it wouldn't kill her like some others had. She stood to live a long, beautiful life with her virus if she would take her meds like she supposed to.

Kaedon on the other hand, was presenting all the symptoms, for it was the same beginning stages she had gone through years ago.

He had done it out of love and not lust, which is why Kaedon wasn't really trippin' out like another person would if they had done it out of lust. But his behavior still scared her. This was not the reality she wanted for Kaedon, but he insisted on sharing it with her.

It's what bonded them together by blood and sacrifice, she thought with an aching heart.

Sacrifice. It's what old man Jake had told her so many years ago. He had sacrificed his dreams of raising a family of his own only to marry a woman and love her immensely even though she couldn't bear him no child.

Kaedon's sacrifice was the result of what happened tonight after the decision he made years ago. He lived with the painful reality that he too could very much contracted H.I.V. He knew the risks and understood them long before he did what he did.

That man's sacrifice was his life for her. To die for her. To share a life with her when he had all the right to walk away.

Chapter 28

It was Amod, his two twin boys, Delani and Demani, Kaedon, Malik, and Alex Junior, a nineteen-year-old sophomore at Florida State University, a star point guard and majoring in computer technology. They were all attending Tyquan's high school championship game with East Gadsden High and leading the startup as a powerful running back. It was his second season playing football and already had a thousand rushing yards, eight touchdowns and two fumble recoveries for a fifteen-year-old 180-pounder. Ty Guy had promising dreams of going pro and he was doing damn good convincing many that he wanted it just as bad as anyone.

The same as with fifteen-year-old Delani and Demani, both wide receivers and fast as lightning on their feet. They had just won their high school championship game the weekend before. Amod was very proud of his boys and was loving how they were turning out to be.

Ciera was so ecstatic that she was the loudest muthafucker in the stands. She was Ty Guy's biggest fan and never missed one game, as well as Malik, who had been there for his little brother every step of the way.

And speaking of which, Malik was still attending school but only for his mother's sake. He was the man on campus, the popular boy who drove the convertible Mustang, and headed his own gang called "STB Clique" which stood for "Secure The Bag". Malik and his ten-man clique were really getting to the money, and they were dangerous individuals also, having already said to be responsible for three murders and two people disappearing and to never be found.

The STB Clique was ruthless as they could, but their main focus was getting money and securing the money bag. No exceptions. They were the new top players in the game. A bunch of young hyenas getting it how they saw fit to their standards.

That evening at the championship game the STB Clique were all present but spread throughout the place. But Malik did have his road dawg with him, Junior was always by his side no matter what.

When Kaedon saw his nephew and his crew mobbing through, they acknowledged one another with a nod. Although Kaedon didn't approve of Malik's gang activities, he still had to respect his mind and let him play his position.

"Look at them," Amod nudged him in the side and Kaedon glanced over at him. "Who do they remind you of?"

"Not us," said Kaedon.

"We had more mercy than they do."

"No we didn't, brah. Back then we didn't spare no one, not even kids. They're moving a whole different way than how we used to. The game has changed now, Amod. You see what's going on. Watch the game," Kaedon gestured toward the football field. He didn't want to talk about Malik and his situation. They'd already had this conversation, and it only led to a result they both didn't like.

"Yeah. You're right. But I know you miss the life just a little bit," said Amod with a smirk.

Kaedon didn't respond to the fact that Amod was right. But that lifestyle had nearly cost him his family. Which is why he always preached to Malik about how he should go about handling his business. Ever since Malik had caught that first body years ago, there was no stopping him. It's been total bloodshed since then.

Malik had become the new prince of the streets, and they loved that young nigga out there.

But he did what he said he would do and that's getting his mother out of the hood. Malik had set her up in a nice four-bedroom house out in the Tallavana gated community by the lake in Havana. With Lance being his connect, Malik was making big moves for a young nigga.

Consequently, it wasn't safe for Ty Guy, and his big brother's street affairs could intervene in his plans.

That's the last thing one would want.

To fuck up Ty Guy's dreams of ever going pro.

***

East Gadsden High lost by two points and instead of being devastated, Ty Guy took it to the chest and agreed to go out to the Waffle House where the rest of the team were on Malik's dime. It was the least Malik could do to lift their spirits up.

While Kaedon was kicking it with Alex Junior and Demani about how he used to clown Amod on the basketball court, Ciera laughed with Ty Guy's girlfriend, Diamond, about something that had nothing to do with sports.

All was going well until Kaedon received a text message from Aryanna telling him to call her.

Being that it was too noisy inside the restaurant, Kaedon excused himself and went outside. He made his way over to the truck and got in behind the wheel. He called his daughter.

When Aryanna picked up on the first ring a premonition of something burdensome washed over Kaedon.

"Kae," said baby girl which was indication that she was mad with him. Aryanna had long ago stopped calling him by his name unless she was mad at him.

"What's up, baby girl?" Kaedon watched as a group of young high school girls walked by his truck.

"Why didn't you tell me I had a brother?" She asked and Kaedon's heart dropped instantly.

"Baby girl, listen to me…" he replied.

"I've been listening to you my whole fuckin' life and all you've been doing is lying. You lied to protect my feelings from the truth. You're not my real father, you're a fuckin' phony! I can't believe you, Kae. I just can't believe you." She sobbed.

"Ary…?" he stammered. "I'm sorry."

"Leave me alone!" she screamed and hung up on him, making Kaedon hurt in a way he never hurt before.

From the inside of the diner, Ciera looked in his direction and smiled, not knowing the turmoil he was going through at that moment.

For a long moment Kaedon sat there with his head hung dejectedly, not wanting to believe what had just happened. It was obvious Aryanna had called him first or else Trenika would have initially made the call. He needed to call his wife. Kaedon was scared of what Aryanna might do now that she knew the truth.

It was bad enough that he'd recently been diagnosed H.I.V. positive but losing his baby girl was worse than anything he could ever face. He called his wife.

Outside the truck, Kaedon noticed that Malik was sending out two of his men to guard his person. Although he was a true family man now, Kaedon was still a gangsta and was considered a threat.

"I just heard, Kaedon." was the first thing Trenika said the instant she answered the phone.

When Kaedon told her what Aryanna said to him she threatened to break her neck.

"How did she find out?" Kaedon asked.

"She friended him on Facebook and Instagram. I looked him up just now too. The kid is some kinda Tik Toker with over 110 million followers. He's a social media sensation, and just the type of kid Ary would be interested in. Now,"

Trenika said with a deep sigh. "I would bet my bottom dollar that baby girl is about to make that boy's life a living hell."

"But how would he know? What woulda brought it on that baby girl –" Kaedon was cut off.

"Stop acting like our daughter isn't the most intelligent young girl we know. Ary's very observant and a great judge of character, and don't much get past her. Knowing her she must've done her homework on the boy and made a connection there. By all means they do resemble each other," Trenika said sourly.

"Go talk to her, Trenika."

"Get home, Kaedon."

"I am."

"Now," she ordered.

After hanging up with his wife, Kaedon went back inside to call it a night with the others. Ciera knew something was wrong, but it was Amod who spoke up first.

He said, "I just need to get home to baby girl."

That brought Malik to a sudden halt with whatever he was doing and turned to his uncle.

"What's wrong with Ary?" He demanded with a hint of malice in his voice.

"I just need to get home," Kaedon repeated.

Without further ado Malik pulled out his car keys. "Let's go see Ary," he said.

Kaedon headed straight for the exit.

Chapter 29

Aryanna was fuming mad as she curled one shapely leg under the other while sitting perched on her bed. She was considering calling her Aunt Jhene or cousin Davida to come get her for the weekend to get away from home. But her thoughts went back to Roman Butler and instead, she logged onto his social media page again.

For Roman, what started off as "a little spam account on Instagram" to entertain himself and friends laid the foundation for an audience of millions on Tik Tok, as well as brand deals with Reebok, Journeys and even Black Enterprise Magazine. Reality television is a career avenue Roman has his eyes on. He says the authenticity of his social media content provides an advantage in presenting himself to the industry.

"He's an actor," muttered Aryanna as she read on. "Roman already is capturing the interest of the entertainment industry…" She was then interrupted by a knock on the bedroom door and glared up in its direction. "What?" she snapped.

"Can I come inside, Ary?" came Trenika's voice.

"No!"

"I wanna talk to you about Roman Butler and who he is."

"Shoulda thought about that years ago, mommy."

"Open the door, Aryanna."

"No," said Aryanna. "Go tell your lies to somebody else!" She got up out of the bed and went over to her stereo system to crank it up. When the room exploded with music Aryanna threw herself back onto her bed.

Moments later, the bedroom door burst inwardly as Trenika kicked it off its hinges. Aryanna bolted up out of her bed in a panic. Stepping over to the stereo system and swiping it off the dresser top, Trenika turned straight at her daughter and slapped fire from her face.

"Ma!" Aryanna bellowed, frightened and holding her face.

"Don't fuckin' mama me now. Talk that fly shit like you just did a second ago!" Trenika grabbed Aryanna by her throat and squeezed. "Don't you ever fix your mouth to disrespect me like that again! You hear me!" She was vicious.

"I'm sorry, mommy!" Aryanna struggled under her restraint as she fought for breath.

Trenika applied pressure upon her daughter. "Do you know what the hell that boy's father took us through?" She fumed.

"Mommy, you're hurting me!" she sobbed.

With a disgusted look on her face, Trenika shoved her daughter away and glared at her darkly.

"It's because of that little boy's father why we are affected with one of the deadliest diseases this world could have ever created. Romell Butler is the reason why I carried so much hatred in my heart most of your life. That man was a master of manipulation, he was a monster. And because of what he did I killed his black ass dead."

"You… killed him?" Aryanna's eyes bulged.

"Damn right I did," said Trenika. "Because that was the only way I could actually live without him haunting our lives."

"You killed somebody…?" Aryanna was shocked.

"Get over it, Ary. He deserved it. Now sit down and let me tell you what I 've been scared to tell you for so long." Trenika moved over to sit down on the edge of the bed.

Scared now, Aryanna had been on the verge of administering her defense techniques on her own mother. But she didn't because she knew that she'd never be forgiven for that.

Reluctantly, she looked down at her broken stereo, feeling the continuous stinging sensation on her face, and stepped over to sit down next to her mother.

"When I met Romell Butler he was the gentlest, caring human being I've ever known..." Trenika began her story as Aryanna listened and heard every painful word with a growing sympathy for the woman who has always been her inspiration.

This was the first time Aryanna ever saw fear in her mother's eyes as she painted her picture of a bad man.

Romell Butler was her mother's misery.

Even in death it was still evident that he had a hold on her mother's fear.

The more she listened, the more Aryanna wondered whether Roman was anything like his father.

When Aryanna first looked at his videos and photos he seemed a bit familiar to her but in an odd way. Then she looked into the history of where he was from and saw that he lives in New Orleans. The coincidence that her mother was from the same place didn't register to her then. But when Aryanna actually looked at Roman, really looked at him and recognized the resemblance, she knew. She knew without a shadow of doubt that the boy that she had begun to admire was her brother somehow.

And after letting the cat out of the bag by confronting her parents about it, Aryanna was struck with the wicked blow of the truth.

That Kaedon wasn't her real father. But he was, and always will be no matter what.

***

Zamon was dozing off in the recliner chair before the TV when there was a knock at his front door. He had been drinking a lot tonight while watching Sports Center and he was pretty tipsy. When the knocking at the door pulled him out of his slumber, he yelled out that he was coming before he even realized he'd said it.

"If I can get the hell into my chair," he muttered as he reached over to take a hold of the sports wheelchair next to the recliner. "Goddamn I'm drunk," he snickered.

After two attempts, Zamon settled himself into the wheelchair and rode smoothly across the living room floor towards the door of his condo apartment.

When asked why he chose a condo apartment instead of a house with his condition, Zamon said he'd always wanted a bachelor's pad of his own. Plus, he had lucked up on a ground floor apartment after Kaedon paid the right price to snatch it from the tenants who'd already purchased it beforehand. The apartment really did fit to Zamon's liking and his neighbors were a lot of help and very respectful.

But now, at nearly one o'clock in the morning, Zamon wondered who in the hell came to visit him at this time.

"Who is it?" He called out.

"It's me, Addison." came the reply.

At the mention of her name, Zamon sobered up fast and reached to open the door. And there she was, Addison Gaskell, in the flesh of her auburn hair cut short over her ears and soft vanilla skin tone with just a sprinkle of freckles dancing across her pretty face. A graduate of Georgetown University and majored in politics, Addison too was a professor at the local college of Clark Atlanta University. And not only that, but she was also his neighbor who lived on the fifth floor.

"I was lonely, and I needed some company," said Addison, stepping into the apartment.

"I'm always available for good company."

"Always," she said.

They entered the sparse but tidy living room where Zamon noticed she had a bottle of wine and a DVD. He asked her what was on the DVD and Addison told him that it was the new Top Gun movie.

"Action-packed." He rubbed his palms together with a smirk on his face. "My type of woman!"

"I'm a sucker for Tom Cruise," she blushed.

He liked it when she blushed like that, it made him feel like he was doing something right.

Of course Addison knew her way around his apartment, for this wasn't her first visit. In the year or so that Zamon had been living there since leaving Kaedon's home, Addison had visited at least fifty times. For a woman of forty-four, she was a beauty and in decent shape. But it was her free-spirit and adventurous nature that clearly fascinated him to the point of him catching feelings.

Both of them were recently divorcees, and together they found a friendship that was worth calling their own. Addison was good to be around, she was the perfect distraction, and she gave Zamon a hope that he couldn't deny.

"A long day, I guess?" said Zamon after she made them both drinks and inserted the DVD into the receiver.

"Not just that but a bad one too," she admitted.

"Wanna talk about it?"

"I don't wanna kill the vibe, Zamon."

He shook his head. "That's what I'm here for, to help you get through things. You could never kill the vibe by doing what's right. Plus, we got Tom Cruise that'll smooth things out if I can't."

"But it's too deep," she replied.

"I'm deeper than deep, baby." Smirked Zamon.

"Okay," she sighed and downed her first cup of wine and turned to face him. "I'm not who you think I am."

"Are you really a man?" Zamon kidded.

She slapped him across the arm with a smile, then her smile quickly changed to a look of earnestness. "My real name is Bailey Louella D'Amelio, and I work for the FBI of the city of Atlanta. I am Special Agent D'Amelio to be exact, and I'm on assignment to investigate one of the most vicious criminals on this coast," she said.

For a very long moment, Zamon just stared at her in absolute befuddlement. "You are serious, aren't you?"

"Yes I am," she said.

"And you're investigating who exactly?" Zamon thought about his twin brother and felt like shit. If she said his brother's name, Zamon was going to punch this bitch's lights out for using him to betray Kaedon.

"It's not your brother or anyone he's associated with on a personal level," she said.

"But it's someone he knows though?"

"But don't deal with it on any basis whatsoever."

"Why are you telling me this?"

"The real truth?"

Zamon sneered at her. "Of course I want the truth, woman! Don't bullshit with me. You know what this could do to me and my brotha? Crush us because he'll think I'm sleeping with the enemy. Because rather you know it or not, Kaedon's very fond of you... whatever - whoever the fuck you are or was pretending to be!" He stated angrily.

"And that's why I told you the truth with who I am, Zamon. I've broken a major rule that could tarnish me for life and lose my career over," she cried.

"Then, why tell me anything?" He demanded.

"Because I love you!" she replied. "I love you. You made me love you. And my case has reached its end. Tomorrow I turn in my report and the case will be done for me. All it takes is for me to take it up to my superior and it's over with for my case, my subject – for us." There were tears in her eyes as she looked at Zamon. "But all you gotta do is say the word and it's done. It's either you or my career. Will you choose me?"

Zamon just looked at her like she'd lost her damn mind.

Of all the things that could be happening at that moment he was faced with this dilemma. One that could get them both killed, to which Zamon wasn't ready to die just yet. He had a decision to make.

One word. That's all he had to say, and it would be over for him. One word, he thought to himself.

Yes or no.

Chapter 30

By the time Kaedon made it back home, it was past two in the morning. When he entered the house, he was only met by Trenika and LuLu. He, Malik, Amod and the twins, were also in tow of the heavy burden of the truth in which Kaedon had shared with them during the ride over.

Of course Amod knew because he was there when Romell died by the hands of the woman who once loved him. It was in his warehouse to which Romell was killed.

But those details weren't shared with Delani and Demani, they only got the simpler version on the matter at hand.

Kaedon kissed his wife and headed straight for Aryanna's bedroom. When he saw the door hanging from the door jamb, he looked back at Trenika. That's when she took him by the hand and pulled him down the hall to their room.

"She's asleep, Kae. Baby girl is emotionally exhausted, and she needs her rest. Talk to her tomorrow."

"Did you tell her?" He asked.

Trenika dropped down onto the big, cushioned loveseat near their massive bed. "Everything. She knows the whole truth now, Kae. It wasn't easy but she deserved to know," she said, her own eyes red from crying not too long ago.

Kaedon sat down onto the bed across from her. "What happened to her bedroom door?"

"I had to pull one of your old moves."

"My old moves?" Kaedon was taken aback by the prospect of what she actually meant.

She told him what went down between her and Aryanna and Kaedon's mouth hit the floor. Then, he shot up to his feet and headed for the door at once. When he entered baby girl's bedroom it was dimly lit from the colorful glow of her computer screen upon her desktop across the room. Soft Jazz music was playing from the sound system sitting partially broken on the dresser. Aryanna got that classical jazz vibe from her mother. She said it's what soothes the soul.

"Baby girl," whispered Kaedon as he neared her bed and placed a gentle kiss upon her cheek.

She didn't even stir. In her arm she cuddled with her life-size Tweety Bird stuffed animal while snoring softly. Aryanna looked so peaceful, but her heart was still broken.

"Just leave her be, Kae," Trenika said from the broken doorway staring in.

Without responding to her, Kaedon kicked off his shoes and climbed into the bed with baby girl. He laid down on the other side of Tweety Bird and watched his daughter sleep without waking her.

"I love you, baby girl. I'm sorry," he murmured. "I'm so sorry I hurt you." Kaedon couldn't help himself, he just had to say something. He needed her to know that he loved her deeply and that he would never hurt her again.

Kaedon watched her sleep for as long as he could before sleep finally swept him underneath.

And he slept fitfully.

***

The next morning when Aryanna opened her eyes, she was instantly astounded by finding Kaedon lying in the bed across from her. She frowned at the thought of what she said to him the night before when she called. She had just made the connection regarding Roman and called her father on speed dial since she already had her phone in hand. She had been so angry with him, so hurt by the truth. That the man she had always known as her hero had been lying to her the whole time.

Her expression softened when she reflected on her life and how much love Kaedon had shown her since day one. What he gave her was something special. Kaedon had changed her life for the better and never once treated her harshly.

"Daddy," whispered Aryanna, pushing softly against his shoulder to wake him up. "Please get up."

Slowly Kaedon's eyes fluttered open as he lay facing her with is head laying upon his left bicep.

"I love you, daddy."

"I love you too, baby girl."

"I'm sorry for what I said last night," she said and plucked him on the nose with a finger. "You're the best thang that could have ever happened to me. You are real, you are true, and you'll always be my father in my eyes."

"Respect. And I'm sorry for lying to you, too," he said.

She shook her head and flipped over on her back to look up at the ceiling. For a moment she didn't say anything and then she yawned and said, "I wanna meet him, daddy."

"That would pose a problem," he warned. "It's dangerous."

"But he's my brother! If what mommy said is true, about Roman not having his mommy or daddy to identify who all was involved that day, then we can get around from hurting him." Aryanna said with another yawn.

At that instant, Kaedon went back to that fateful day when Trenika murdered Romell and Tazzy took the life of Layla. The son was left to the care of his grandmother, then she died from heart failure and nobody else would take him. Roman ended up going into the system and then several years later an older cousin stepped up and took custody of him.

Roman's life had been saved from the government by another relative who believed in his future.

The kid had so much to live for now.

"I wanna meet him, daddy. I want Roman to know that he still has family who cares," said Aryanna.

"Okay." Kaedon grunted.

Aryanna turned her head to face him. "Are you gonna take me to meet him?"

"When do you wanna go?"

She leaned up on one elbow. "Next week, Friday. I want to spend that whole weekend with him. Plus, I miss Aunt Jhene and Davida and Rhonda and Grandma Cors –"

"Okay okay okay, with your buggin' ass!" said Kaedon.

"Shut up, old man!" She shoved him.

"What?" Kaedon looked over at her for a second then he pounced on her, tickling her ribs. Aryanna shrieked loudly and laughed deliriously as she tried to get away from him.

A moment later, both Malik and Trenika came rushing to the bedroom doorway and looked inside. Trenika stood there smiling as she watched her husband and daughter at play. They had made up and all was well.

Fifteen minutes later, they were all in the spacious kitchen downstairs eating a variety of breakfast. Malik sat close to Aryanna giving her all the attention she desired. Then Jade came knocking and little Delani was immediately smitten by the girl who has been Aryanna's best friend since day one. Amod looked like he wanted to intervene in their little innocent flirting back and forth until Trenika gave him that eye not to do it.

Another hour rolled by and Aryanna was behind the wheel of her mother's car while she sat riding shotgun coaching her with Jade in the backseat. Every chance she got Aryanna's mother gave her driving lessons and baby girl was getting better every course.

"Did you tell her yet," said Jade after stopping at a gas station and Trenika went inside.

Aryanna looked back at her friend. "No."

"You know you can't hold out too long before she does find out, Ary. and you damn sure don't want your father to find out first or he's gonna really trip."

"He's gonna do that anyway," said Aryanna sourly.

Jade didn't respond when she noticed Trenika headed back to the car.

Both girls watched as Trenika proceeded to pump gas into the car while looking stunning as she always does. They were on their way to visit with Doneica, who was now preparing to attend the University of Southern California School of Cinematic Arts. She was currently interning for a management company and joined a Clark Atlanta University acting program that encouraged her to want to go to California. But today, Donecia wanted them to come out and watch her perform in a play that was being viewed at the college.

"Roman would love her," said Aryanna.

"Roman?" said Jade curiously. "Who is Roman?" she asked.

Aryanna and her mother exchanged a glance. Jade noticed this and knew automatically that they were holding something back.

"Who is Roman?" She repeated.

Chapter 31

It was three days later when Zamon found himself being lifted up into the truck of his brother's by his brother. It was a beautiful sunny afternoon, so beautiful that Zamon wanted to relax by the pool and drink champagne. And of course, give Kaedon the surprising news.

But before any of that could happen the unexpected presence of Zamon's father interrupted their moment. At the sight of the old man Zamon saw something on him that made Zamon worry. Hezachi Newman looked every bit of his seventy-five years old. The man didn't look to good and Zamon had a bad feeling that he knew what it was.

Also accompanying Zamon's father was Stephen Owens, who was Melody's brother and Zamon's good friend.

Standing in the doorway of the passenger side of the truck, Kaedon watched as the old man approached the truck.

"Son," said Hezachi Newman, his eyes sad and his voice thick with emotion. "It's about your mama."

"What's wrong?" Zamon heard the tremor in his voice.

Hezachi said, "She's had a stroke and I think you need to come and say goodbye before it's too late."

"Goodbye?" A deep feeling of dread came over Zamon.

"Sometimes you never know with these things."

Zamon held his father's gaze, then he turned to his brother, and all the answer he needed was in his eyes.

"Go see your mama, brah," Kaedon told him.

"Come with me?" Zamon asked.

"Of course."

Hours later Zamon was sitting at his mother's bedside weeping sorrowfully while everybody was outside the room. He wanted to be with her alone to make his amends.

When he and Melody divorced, Zamon pretty much cut everybody off except for Kaedon and his family. He moved out of the house and changed his number. He hadn't spoken to his parents in years. The only reason his father found him was through Kaedon after following him for two days. When Kaedon learned this he was hot, but he remained humbled about it, and thought to himself that he would have done the same thing.

Now that he was in front of his mother, Zamon saw how much she'd aged over the years. She was three years older than her husband. Rose Newman and Zamon hadn't had a good memorable moment the last time they met. They had a big disagreement where Zamon left her in tears. Zamon regretted ever hurting his mother and wished he could take it all back.

"You've come," came the hoarseness of his mother's voice that sent Zamon's head snapping upward.

"Ma," he cried. "Mama I'm sorry. Please forgive me."

"I knew you'd come, son. Mama ain't doing too well. But don't worry your poor little heart, I'll be alright with my Lord if he chooses to come get me." Her words came slow and weakly.

"No, mama. You're gonna live through this." Zamon was crying openly now as he reached up to take her hand. Rose's hand was frail and brittle looking and cold to the touch. "You just hold on and be strong," he said.

"Hold on... That was my song, wasn't it? I'm surprised you remembered it, Hezachi," she said.

Zamon stiffened at her calling him by his father's name. "Huh?"

"Hold on, change is coming. Hold on…" Rose sang. "Don't worry 'bout a thang!" She smiled weakly and closed her beautiful light brown eyes.

"Mama? Ma?" Zamon panicked. "Ma. Wake up!" he stressed.

"… Don't worry 'bout a thang," Rose sang some more and smiled her last smile. "Everything's gone be alright…" she finished.

Mama was finally gone.

And Zamon howled like a wounded animal as he clung to the hand of his mother. And once again, his sanity took another wrong turn.

***

Tazzy was squatted down on one knee shaking a pair of blue dice in her hand while talking shit as they all occupied the curb outside Von's mama's house. Lying on the ground in front of her was a pile of cash held down by the weight of her Glock.

"You niggaz thought I've lost my game, huh!" said Tazzy, dressed in a pair of tight-fitting Dickie pants, designer wife beater, and Air Maxes fresh out the box. "I'ma have yo niggaz going to get your light bill money in a minute."

"Cuz, shoot the damn dice and stop talkin' shit!" Humble replied with irritation.

"Keep talkin' and I'll make you up the ante," she quipped.

"Whatever you wanna do, cuz." He shrugged.

With a smirk on her face, Tazzy reached inside her pocket and retrieved a big thick roll of cash. She tossed the money at Humble's Converse sneakers and said, "That's ten grand right there, big mouth. Put up or shut up, cuz!"

"Oohh!" some of the other homies standing around them sang in unison at the challenge.

Humble reached into his pocket and brought out his own bank of cash money just as Lance pulled up on the scene in his Benz truck.

Lance hit the horn and hung out the driver side window. "I need to holla at you, my nigga," he replied with a smirk on his face. "What's that, three-dice C-low?"

"You know it, cuz!" Von answered as he approached the truck and gave Lance some love.

"You lucky, cuz!" Tazzy blew a kiss at Humble as she collected her money and pistol. Then she turned to her right-hand man Po'Boi and said, "Let's roll, cuz."

As both Tazzy and her man got into the truck, Lance informed the remainder of the homies that he'll have her back soon enough to win their money. Humble gave him the middle finger and the truck sped away with Tazzy still talking shit and laughing.

"What's crackin', Lance? I heard you just opened up that new nightclub over off the beach, cuz," said Tazzy.

"Club Revolt," Lance replied.

"Yeah. That's a good look, cuz. One of my old comrades had that spot and crapped out. But I think you're gonna do some justice with that one. How is Quanda?"

"She's good. But check it, Taz. I'm not here to talk socially with you," Lance glanced over at her as Tazzy identified the seriousness in his voice.

No longer good-natured but wary now, Tazzy turned her body fully around to face Lance. With her back against the passenger door, it gave Po'Boi all the reason to be more alert to watch the traffic around them.

"What's going on, Lance?" Tazzy asked.

"It's about your brotha, Zee."

"What about him?"

Lance didn't answer her right away and Tazzy saw something flash across his face.

"Okay, since you don't wanna talk, cuz," said Tazzy before reaching to get her cell phone. "I'll call Zee myself."

"He won't answer," he told her.

"He will for me," she stated firmly as she proceeded to dial Zamon's number. Then Lance reached over to place a hand on top of hers to stop her from making the call.

"Zamon is dead, Taz. He killed himself sometime late last night," said Lance.

"No!" Stop it, Lance!" Tazzy cried out and punched him in the shoulder. "Don't say that! Don't play with me like that."

"I'm not playing," he said.

Snatching her gaze away from him, Tazzy turned back to her phone and finished dialing the phone. Her eyes were welling up with tears of sorrow. She could barely see the numbers on the phone but completed the call. When it began to ring she felt herself begin to burn with depression.

"Sis," came Kaedon's voice picking up on the fourth ring and causing Tazzy to grow scared.

"Is it true, Kae? Please tell me it's not true, cuz. Where is Zee?" She pleaded with her brother.

Hesitantly, Kaedon sighed and murmured, "He's gone, sis."

"Gone where, Kae?"

"He's… dead," cried Kaedon miserably. "Zamon is dead."

Hearing her brother say it out his own mouth and hearing the pain in his cries is what shattered all that hardness she was trying to hold on to. Tazzy fell against Lance's shoulder and sobbed like a brokenhearted child. She clung to him desperately, breaking to pieces with every fallen tear.

In the backseat Po'Boi sent out a message to the third-in-command to deliver the bad news.

The queen was out of commission for the time being.

She was all broken up. That was dangerous.

Chapter 32

A week later, Kaedon sat outside on the curb before the Newman's residence in Albany, Ga. smoking a fat blunt of weed. He was still dressed in his black Ralph Lauren purple label suit and tie as he thought about his dead brother. Never in his life had he imagined ever burying his twin brother. They were supposed to grow old together and die from old age. But he guessed God had another plan in mind.

After sitting outside alone for a while his Aunt Amy and Jhene comes outside fuckin' with him on some sympathetic shit again.

"I said I don't want to be fuckin' bothered," he snapped.

"We're just trying to help, Kaedon," Jhene reasoned.

Kaedon rose up to his feet and began walking up the street along the sidewalk.

If he could say anything to Zamon right now Kaedon would punch him in his face and called him a fuckin' coward for playing himself like that. Here he was, he got all these people there for him crying their eyes out and talking about how good of a man he was. Kaedon didn't want to hear that shit and separated himself from them all. He just wanted to be alone.

For about ten minutes, he walked around the neighborhood smoking his blunt and trying damn hard to keep his own tears at bay. Then he happened upon a neighborhood park where he spotted a young black kid shooting hoops with a deflated basketball. Kaedon stood there watching the kid for a minute, lost in thought and wondering where he goes from there.

His cellphone rang and he reached into his suit coat pocket to retrieve it. It was Tazzy calling. Kaedon looked out towards the lone kid and caught him gazing out after him.

"What's up?" He answered.

"Are you alright?" Tazzy asked.

"That's a dumb question, sis," he grumbled.

She hesitated, said, "You need me to do anything?"

As he stared out at the kid again he told Tazzy what he really needed and disconnected the call.

With a troubled breath, he stepped through the entrance gate of the park while removing his jacket and tie. Then, he stepped onto the court and approached the kid.

"Wanna one on one, little man?" Kaedon replied.

"It won't be fair on you when I beat you with a deflated ball," he said with a smirk.

"Isn't that right? What's your name, little man?"

"Jayden."

"A'ight, Jayden. Shot for shot. I saw you shootin' the ball a minute ago and I was impressed."

"It's what I do," Jayden said with a sense of confidence that shone in his beady little eyes.

"But are you any good with a giant heavyweight guarding you?" Kaedon challenged him.

"I can manage." Jayden knew just the right words to say.

"What position do you play, Jayden?"

"Point guard," he said proudly.

"And how old are you?"

"Eleven."

"Good. After I embarrass you on this court today, I'ma hashtag 'I outshot eleven-year-old Jayden'."

"We all can dream, right? You go first." Jayden passed him the ball with immense power for a little scrawny kid who was no bigger than a number 2 pencil.

From half court Kaedon turned toward the basket, got into his shooting stance, spun the ball between his hands, and shot it from the distance. The basketball made it into the hoop hitting nothing but net.

"Good shot. But I can do better," said Jayden.

"I know. Your shot, Lebron!"

At being called one of his most favorite players in the NBA, Jayden hustled to go retrieve the basketball back and took up his position in the same spot.

When Kaedon noticed movement out his peripheral he turned to see a cute slim redbone chick standing just inside the entrance gate of the park. It wasn't hard to recognize the resemblance that Jayden shared with the woman. This was the kid's mother and she had come to investigate the man whom her son had suddenly become associated with.

At the sound of the ball hitting the backboard Kaedon turned to witness the successful shot.

"And you say you could do better than my shot," he said.

"I made it, didn't I?" Jayden retorted.

From behind him Kaedon heard his mother clapping with encouragement as the kid grinned cockily.

"Oh. I see what's going on," Kaedon was not about to be shown up by this kid in front of his mother. So when he got the ball next Kaedon took his position from a side pocket shot and missed.

Jayden laughed at him and made the same shot.

***

"He said to go find a basketball and buy it," Tazzy said to Jhene and Aryanna who was occupying the car with her as she drove.

"Do we even know where we're going?" Aryanna asked as she stuck her head forward between the two women's shoulders up front.

194

Jhene said she remembered seeing a super Wal-Mart shopping center in a plaza east of Main Street where they had come from the burial site earlier.

"What would he want a basketball for?" asked Jhene.

"What would anyone want with a basketball, auntie?" Aryanna sat back in her seat in the back. "Maybe he wants to go somewhere and shoot some ball to get his mind off his brotha. Daddy is hurting and he needs the distraction," she said, removing her phone from her purse.

"That's a reasonable excuse," Jhene replied.

It was then that Tazzy reminded them that Kaedon had always been athletic but never played organized sports because of his responsibilities at home. He did well, and then after finally joining the basketball team in junior high, his coach told him that if he worked hard he could attend college on a basketball scholarship somewhere.

"But he never went to college though," Jhene interjected with a look of interest.

"That was a foreign concept to Kae," said Aryanna knowingly as if she really knew.

In the tenth grade, Kaedon moved out of Grandma Lillie's house into the house with his cousin Mario and his two siblings. His granny made him a wise kid then, to which he cast caution aside and made the basketball team. Amazingly, Kaedon was soon ranked number two in the state for rebounds. He went from being a nobody to a somebody. The local *hood stars* bought him expensive shoes, the girls chased after him, and Kaedon became the golden kid.

"Daddy was the man," grinned Aryanna mischievously.

"Kaedon had made plans to attend Florida State University and crush the basketball camp - but all that changed when Twan got locked up and facing the rest of his life in prison."

"What happened?" Jhene asked.

"At sixteen years old, Kaedon's life took a drastic turn for the worse," said Tazzy. "To keep his loyalty to his friend he had to do some thangs that not even himself would want to speak on anymore. But just know during his eleventh-grade year in high school, is where Kaedon really came to a realization how gangsta he was."

"Even before then Kae was in the streets, but only went to school to satisfy his grandmother Lillie."

"I wished I could have met her," said Aryanna softly.

"As we all, baby girl," said Tazzy. "As we all."

They eventually located the Wal-Mart as both Jhene and Aryanna ran inside to purchase the basketball. Afterwards, they hurried back to the neighborhood and looked around for the park Kaedon said he would be. When they found him, he was in the company of a young kid and another woman.

"Who is she?" Jhene instantly became protective over her best friend's husband and was glaring in the direction of the other equally pretty woman.

"Calm your nerves, cuz. It's not even that serious." Tazzy parked the car at the curb outside the neighborhood park and opened the door to get out.

Aryanna, with the brand-new brown leather Spalding basketball still encased in its cardboard confinement, got out of the car next and went into the park.

Kaedon rose up from where he was sitting in the middle of the basketball court. He nodded solemnly at his daughter as she handed him the basketball. Then he made the introductions introducing Jayden and his mother, Brianna, whom in turn introduced the others in the same grace.

"And this is yours, little man." Kaedon then extended the brand-new basketball to Jayden.

"Really?" The kid gasped in shock.

Kaedon nodded.

When Jayden looked at his mother for confirmation, her smile was all the answer he needed.

"Thank you Kaedon," the boy cried as he took the ball slowly, admiring the gift with absolute awe. "Thank you so much. You must know I'd beat you today. Did I win the ball?" he asked slyly.

"He beat you, daddy?" Aryanna was surprised by this.

"I let him win," Kaedon said.

"Yeah, right." Tazzy wasn't convinced and took little Jayden's side against her brother's.

"Whatever. And no, you didn't win the ball, Jayden. I saw that you needed a better one and I made sure you got one. And since all y'all tryna insult my game," Kaedon took the ball back and freed it from its confinement. "I'll take on all five of y'all's asses and whip you like y'all stole something," he challenged.

Jhene began removing her pumps and her jewelry at once. Tazzy took off her Calvin Klein jacket, and Jayden restrung his shoelaces to perform for battle.

"Oh. You're about to get it now, daddy," said Aryanna, excited to see her father back in his groove.

Chapter 33

It was another two weeks when Roman Butler glanced back over his shoulder towards the basement stairs at the sound of the door opening. Then, someone began descending the stairs and Roman watched with silent reproach as someone other than his cousin Dana came into view.

Roman swiveled his chair completely round as the sight of the girl from his social media friend group revealed herself. His heart begins to thump brutally in his chest. He stood up and watched as the girl approached him with confident strides. This was the first time he ever had a girl down in his laboratory and Roman did not approve of such an intrusion.

"What are you doing down here?" Roman demanded.

"To meet my little brother," she said with a grin. Then she extended her delicate hand, her fingernails painted a shade of a shiny peach color to compliment her skin tone. "As you already know me, I'm Aryanna Mahagani Smith."

"And how are you my sister?" Roman replied, the tone in which he used was filled with skepticism.

"Simple. Our father, Romell Butler, was messing with both of our mothers around the same time. I'm one year older than you, by way of Romell finding comfort in your mother after my mother left him to go move away," said Aryanna.

"But why?" Asked Roman. "Why did she move away?"

"In life, some things never work out the way you expect them to. Our father was a busy man, and I never got the opportunity to personally meet him."

"It's because he was a thug," said Roman.

"What?" She paused.

Roman reclaimed his seat positioned in front of his laptop computer, which was surrounded by four other larger screens stationed around the long desktop. The whole setup looked like something only a nerd or some computer savvy freak of a hacker would devote his energy on. What lie before them was not only costly but dangerously delicate property that came with very strict handling.

"My father was a thug. It was because of him that my mother died. I can't say that I hate the man, because that was a long time ago. But what I did hate was having to lose my grandma and then put into a foster home. That place was a nightmare," he shook his head wearily.

That's when Aryanna looked around the room and spotted a blue plastic chair and went over to get it.

"Let's talk," she sat down in the chair before him.

"I thought that's what we were doing." He shrugged.

"You tell me your life and I'll tell you mine. No bullshit. No holding back. If you cry then that's okay too, but I am not leaving this fuckin' basement until we are on the same page," Aryanna said, crossing her thick, firm legs lady-like and giving him her undivided attention.

For the next several hours that's exactly what they did, sparing one another anything as they cried together, laughed, and got to know each other on a deeper level.

In the process, Aryanna learned his strengths and weaknesses, but overall Roman was an interesting subject. Her estranged brother was allergic to seafood and Aspirin, he didn't drink milk or eat mustard, but he was one helluva gamer and loved computers which was blatantly obvious.

The whole afternoon had flown by, and it was sometime after 9:00 that evening the two of them emerged from the basement into a living room full of people. Roman acknowledged his cousin Dana, who was his legal guardian now, and she was grinning from ear to ear while nursing a glass of wine. There were two men present, whom Roman now knew as Kaedon and Malik, added with Aryanna's best friend Jade. The energy in the room was lively and it wasn't hard to see that everybody was in their element.

"So I take it you two have survived the first challenge, eh," said Dana, tall, dark and attractive, and with a pair of lips one would die for.

"What challenge?" Aryanna asked curiously.

It was Kaedon who responded. "The one where you both come to an understanding of who you are."

"And the second one?" asked Roman.

"Bonding," said Dana. "A bond that only siblings could achieve despite the circumstances." Her words made Kaedon think about his brother Zamon and pray that Aryanna didn't have to go through what he'd gone through. Her heart was too good to be broken by the crushing pain of losing a brother.

Epilogue

(9 Years Later)

Baby girl was a nervous wreck as she stood in line with her graduation cap and gown on. This was her moment, and Aryanna couldn't for the life of her stay still from the anxiousness that she was experiencing. She was graduating from Clark Atlanta University, majoring in business and accounting; the president of her AKA sorority sisterhood and ready to begin her new life as a successful woman. When Aryanna searched the boisterous crowd of the humungous auditorium for her family, her smile lit up the room when she spotted her father and mother cheering her on. Everybody who loved and cared for her was there and Aryanna couldn't be a more happier woman than she was at that moment.

These past nine years have been a very trying experience, but Aryanna progressed through it all. She had grown to become a strong black woman of distinction. There was no denying the powerful woman she was still yet to come.

As the line of graduates representing the class of '23 moved forward, she turned back to her mother for encouragement. Trenika gave her two thumbs up and blew her a kiss. Kaedon was crying like a bitch. He was so pitiful standing there in her pink and green sororities colors with her face printed on the T-shirt he was wearing in honor of her.

"Aryanna Smith!" the dean of the students announced throughout the large room of people.

Aryanna stepped up to the platform, walked across the stage to receive her diploma.

"Congratulations, Ms. Smith. I wish you further success," said the school's president, Martha Bastien.

"Thank you," Aryanna grinned beautiful as she took her diploma and the woman's hand.

Then she turned toward the crowd and presented the certification in the air.

"We did it, baby! We did it!" she screamed and did a little dance that made the room roar in clamorous cheer.

Next, Aryanna approached the other end of the platform stage and smiled when she saw Malik standing there waiting for her to meet him at the other end. Then when she finally made it to him, and he took her hand; Malik got down on one knew and produced a huge 5 carat diamond ring that shined like the sun. Every breath in the room suddenly inhaled. Kaedon thought he was about to have a heart attack.

"Who do you love Ary?" Malik looked up at her with promise.

Trenika felt her knees go weak.

"You," Aryanna vowed. "I love you Malik."

Both Kaedon and his wife hugged one another close.

"For how long?" he replied.

A momentary pause.

"Forever," she said. "Always and forever."

And then he slipped the diamond ring onto her finger making Aryanna cry and blush with pride at the same time. Her secret was finally out, her love was real and belonged in the heart that no other man could entrust.

The heart of a gangsta who overflowed with A THUGGISH PASSION for her that would forever be hers.

THE END

Lock Down Publications and Ca$h Presents
Assisted Publishing Packages

Due to an increase in the price of services we have increased our prices. The prices below reflect the price increase as of 11/1/24.

BASIC PACKAGE	UPGRADED PACKAGE
$699	**$1000**
Editing	Typing
Cover Design	Editing
Formatting	Cover Design
	Formatting
	Upload eBooks to Amazon
	Upload Paperback to Amazon
ADVANCE PACKAGE	**LDP SUPREME PACKAGE**
$1,400	**$1,700**
Typing	Typing
Editing (line editing/content)	Editing (line editing/content)
Cover Design	Cover Design
Formatting	Formatting
Copyright Registration	Copyright Registration
Proofreading	Proofreading
Upload eBooks to Amazon	Set up Amazon Account
Upload Paperback to Amazon	Upload eBooks to Amazon
	Upload Paperback to Amazon
	Advertise on LDP's Amazon and Facebook Page

***Other services available upon request.
Additional charges may apply

Lock Down Publications
P.O. Box 944
Stockbridge, GA 30281-9998
Phone: 470 303-9761
Email: lockdownpublications@gmail.com

Submission Guideline

Submit the first three chapters of your completed manuscript to ldpsubmissions@gmail.com. In the subject line add **Your Book's Title**. The manuscript must be in a Word Doc file and sent as an attachment. Document should be in Times New Roman, double spaced, and in size 12 font. Also, provide your synopsis and full contact information. If sending multiple submissions, they must each be in a separate email.

Have a story but no way to send it electronically? You can still submit to LDP/Ca$h Presents. Send in the first three chapters, written or typed, of your completed manuscript to:

LDP: Submissions Dept
P.O. Box 944
Stockbridge, GA 30281-9998

DO NOT send original manuscript. Must be a duplicate.
Provide your synopsis and a cover letter containing your full contact information.

Thanks for considering LDP and Ca$h Presents.

NEW RELEASES

BLOODLINE OF A SAVAGE 1,2&3
THESE VICIOUS STREETS 1,2&3
RELENTLESS GOON
RELENTLESS GOON 2
BY PRINCE A. TAUHID

THE BUTTERFLY MAFIA 1-3
BY FUMIYA PAYNE

A THUG'S STREET PRINCESS 1,2&3
BY MEESHA

CITY OF SMOKE 1& 2
BY MOLOTTI

STEPPERS 1,2&3
THE REAL BADDIES OF CHI-RAQ
BY KING RIO

THE LANE 1&2
BY KEN-KEN SPENCE

THUG OF SPADES 1,2&3
LOVE IN THE TRENCHES 2
CORNER BOY CHRONICLES
BY COREY ROBINSON

TIL DEATH 3
BY ARYANNA

THE BIRTH OF A GANGSTER 4
BY DELMONT PLAYER

PRODUCT OF THE STREETS 1&2
BY DEMOND "MONEY" ANDERSON

NO TIME FOR ERROR
BY KEESE

MONEY HUNGRY DEMONS 1,2&3
BY TRANAY ADAMS

HUNGRY FOR MONEY 1&2
BY SLIMBOS

A THUGGISH PASSION
KILLAZ ON STANDBY 1&2
LAND OF DA HOOLIGANZ 1,2&3
FRESH OFF DA PORCH
BY IRA B.

COUNTDOWN OF A KILLA 1&2
GUNS DOWN, BOTTOMS UP 1&2
SEX, MURDA AND GOD
BY LO-LIFE

THE LEVEL UP 1&2
BY LUXURY KING

FO'EVA ROLLIN' 1&2
BY ASSA RAYMOND BAKER

HUB CITY MENACE 1&2
BY J. WHITE

KILLA CREW
DYING FOR LIKES
BY ARYANNA

A THUGGISH PASSION 2 | IRA B

IF YOU CROSS ME ONCE 6
ANGEL 5
By Anthony Fields

IMMA DIE BOUT MINE 5
By Aryanna

A THUGS STREET PRINCESS 3
EMBRACING THE LOVE OF A BOSS
By Meesha

PRODUCT OF THE STREETS 3
By Demond Money Anderson

STANDING ON HER BUSINESS
BY DG SANTANA

GET IT IN SLUGS 1&2
B. STALLS

CORNER BOYS 2
By Corey Robinson

THE MURDER QUEENS 6&7
By Michael Gallon

CITY OF SMOKE 3
By Molotti

CONFESSIONS OF A DOPEBOY
By Nicholas Lock

TENDER
BY KHUFU

THA TAKEOVER
By Keith Chandler

BETRAYAL OF A G 2
By Ray Vinci

CRIME BOSS 4
By Playa Ray

Coming Soon from Lock Down Publications/Ca$h Presents

RAN OFF ON THE PLUG 2 by **PAPER BOI RARI**
STREET REDEMPTION by **TONY DANIELS**
SAVAGE FAMILY EMPIRE by **PRINCE TAUHID**
BAD BITCHES WIT' GUNZ by **DIESEL**
THE SINGLE LADIES by **DIESEL**
COKE BY THE TRUCKLOAD by **DIESEL**
PROBLEM SOLVED by **DIESEL**
TIPPIN' THE SCALES by **DIESEL**
OPPS CRY TOO by **SAYNOMORE**
A GANGSTA'S KARMA by **FLAME**

AVAILABLE NOW

RESTRAINING ORDER 1 & 2
By **CA$H & Coffee**

LOVE KNOWS NO BOUNDARIES 1-3
By **Coffee**

RAISED AS A GOON I, II, III & IV
BRED BY THE SLUMS I, II, III
BLAST FOR ME I & II
ROTTEN TO THE CORE I II III
A BRONX TALE I, II, III
DUFFLE BAG CARTEL I II III IV V VI
HEARTLESS GOON I II III IV V
A SAVAGE DOPEBOY I II
DRUG LORDS I II III
CUTTHROAT MAFIA I II
KING OF THE TRENCHES
By **Ghost**

LAY IT DOWN I & II
LAST OF A DYING BREED I II
BLOOD STAINS OF A SHOTTA I & II III
By **Jamaica**

LOYAL TO THE GAME I II III
LIFE OF SIN I, II III
By **TJ & Jelissa**

IF LOVING HIM IS WRONG…I & II
LOVE ME EVEN WHEN IT HURTS I II III
By **Jelissa**

A THUGGISH PASSION 2 | IRA B

PUSH IT TO THE LIMIT
By **Bre' Hayes**

BLOODY COMMAS I & II
SKI MASK CARTEL I, II & III
KING OF NEW YORK I II, III IV V
RISE TO POWER I II III
COKE KINGS I II III IV V
BORN HEARTLESS I II III IV
KING OF THE TRAP I II
By **T.J. Edwards**

WHEN THE STREETS CLAP BACK I & II III
THE HEART OF A SAVAGE I II III IV
MONEY MAFIA I II
LOYAL TO THE SOIL I II III
By **Jibril Williams**

A DISTINGUISHED THUG STOLE MY HEART I - III
LOVE SHOULDN'T HURT I II III IV
RENEGADE BOYS 1-4
PAID IN KARMA 1-3
SAVAGE STORMS 1-3
AN UNFORESEEN LOVE 1-3
BABY, I'M WINTERTIME COLD 1-3
A THUG'S STREET PRINCESS 1&2
By **Meesha**

CUM FOR ME 1-8
An LDP Erotica Collaboration

BLOOD OF A BOSS 1-5
SHADOWS OF THE GAME
TRAP BASTARD
By **Askari**

211

A GANGSTER'S CODE 1-3
A GANGSTER'S SYN 1-3
THE SAVAGE LIFE 1-3
CHAINED TO THE STREETS 1-3
BLOOD ON THE MONEY 1-3
A GANGSTA'S PAIN 1-3
BEAUTIFUL LIES AND UGLY TRUTHS
CHURCH IN THESE STREETS
By **J-Blunt**

THE STREETS BLEED MURDER 1-3
THE HEART OF A GANGSTA 1-3
By **Jerry Jackson**

WHEN A GOOD GIRL GOES BAD
By **Adrienne**

THE COST OF LOYALTY 1-3
By **Kweli**

BRIDE OF A HUSTLA 1-3
THE FETTI GIRLS 1-3
CORRUPTED BY A GANGSTA 1-4
BLINDED BY HIS LOVE
THE PRICE YOU PAY FOR LOVE 1-3
DOPE GIRL MAGIC 1-3
By **Destiny Skai**

A KINGPIN'S AMBITION
A KINGPIN'S AMBITION II
I MURDER FOR THE DOUGH
By **Ambitious**

A DOPEBOY'S PRAYER
By **Eddie "Wolf" Lee**

TRUE SAVAGE 1-7
DOPE BOY MAGIC 1-3
MIDNIGHT CARTEL 1-3
CITY OF KINGZ 1&2
NIGHTMARE ON SILENT AVE
THE PLUG OF LIL MEXICO 1&2
CLASSIC CITY
By **Chris Green**

LOVE & CHASIN' PAPER
By **Qay Crockett**

THE KING CARTEL 1-3
By **Frank Gresham**

THESE NIGGAS AIN'T LOYAL 1-3
By **Nikki Tee**

GANGSTA SHYT 1-3
By **CATO**

THE ULTIMATE BETRAYAL
By **Phoenix**

BOSS'N UP 1-3
By **Royal Nicole**

I LOVE YOU TO DEATH
By **Destiny J**

BROOKLYN HUSTLAZ
By **Boogsy Morina**

GANGSTA CITY
By **Teddy Duke**

TO DIE IN VAIN
SINS OF A HUSTLA
By **ASAD**

I RIDE FOR MY HITTA
I STILL RIDE FOR MY HITTA
By **Misty Holt**

A GANGSTER'S REVENGE 1-4
THE BOSS MAN'S DAUGHTERS 1-5
A SAVAGE LOVE 1&2
BAE BELONGS TO ME 1&2
A HUSTLER'S DECEIT 1-3
WHAT BAD BITCHES DO 1-3
SOUL OF A MONSTER 1-3
KILL ZONE
A DOPE BOY'S QUEEN 1-3
TIL DEATH 1-3
IMMA DIE BOUT MINE 1-5
By **Aryanna**

BROOKLYN ON LOCK 1 & 2
By **Sonovia**

A DRUG KING AND HIS DIAMOND 1-3
A DOPEMAN'S RICHES
HER MAN, MINE'S TOO 1&2
CASH MONEY HO'S
THE WIFEY I USED TO BE 1&2
PRETTY GIRLS DO NASTY THINGS
By **Nicole Goosby**

THE STREETS ARE CALLING
By **Duquie Wilson**

LIPSTICK KILLAH 1-3
CRIME OF PASSION 1-3
FRIEND OR FOE 1-3
By **Mimi**

TRAPHOUSE KING 1-3
KINGPIN KILLAZ 1-3
STREET KINGS 1&2
PAID IN BLOOD 1&2
CARTEL KILLAZ 1-3
DOPE GODS 1&2
By **Hood Rich**

STEADY MOBBN' 1-3
THE STREETS STAINED MY SOUL 1-3
By **Marcellus Allen**

WHO SHOT YA 1-3
SON OF A DOPE FIEND 1-4
HEAVEN GOT A GHETTO 1&2
SKI MASK MONEY 1&2
By **Renta**

GORILLAZ IN THE BAY 1-4
TEARS OF A GANGSTA 1/&2
3X KRAZY 1&2
STRAIGHT BEAST MODE 1&2
By **DE'KARI**

TRIGGADALE 1-3
MURDA WAS THE CASE 1-3
By **Elijah R. Freeman**

MARRIED TO A BOSS 1-3
By **Destiny Skai & Chris Green**

SLAUGHTER GANG 1-3
RUTHLESS HEART 1-3
By **Willie Slaughter**

GOD BLESS THE TRAPPERS 1-3
THESE SCANDALOUS STREETS 1-3
FEAR MY GANGSTA 1-5
THESE STREETS DON'T LOVE NOBODY 1-2
BURY ME A G 1-5
A GANGSTA'S EMPIRE 1-4
THE DOPEMAN'S BODYGAURD 1&2
THE REALEST KILLAZ 1-3
THE LAST OF THE OGS 1-3
By **Tranay Adams**

KINGZ OF THE GAME 1-7
CRIME BOSS 1-4
By **Playa Ray**

FUK SHYT
By **Blakk Diamond**

DON'T F#CK WITH MY HEART 1&2
By **Linnea**

ADDICTED TO THE DRAMA 1-3
IN THE ARM OF HIS BOSS
By **Jamila**

LOYALTY AIN'T PROMISED 1&2
By **Keith Williams**

FOREVER GANGSTA 1&2
GLOCKS ON SATIN SHEETS 1&2
By **Adrian Dulan**

YAYO 1-4
A SHOOTER'S AMBITION 1&2
BRED IN THE GAME
By **S. Allen**

TRAP GOD 1-3
RICH $AVAGE 1-3
MONEY IN THE GRAVE 1-3
CARTEL MONEY
By **Martell Troublesome Bolden**

TOE TAGZ 1-4
LEVELS TO THIS SHYT 1&2
IT'S JUST ME AND YOU
By **Ah'Million**

KINGPIN DREAMS 1-3
RAN OFF ON DA PLUG
By **Paper Boi Rari**

THE STREETS MADE ME 1-3
By **Larry D. Wright**

CONFESSIONS OF A GANGSTA 1-4
CONFESSIONS OF A JACKBOY 1-3
CONFESSIONS OF A HITMAN
By **Nicholas Lock**

I'M NOTHING WITHOUT HIS LOVE
SINS OF A THUG
TO THE THUG I LOVED BEFORE
A GANGSTA SAVED XMAS
IN A HUSTLER I TRUST
By **Monet Dragun**

A THUGGISH PASSION 2 | IRA B

QUIET MONEY 1-3
THUG LIFE 1-3
EXTENDED CLIP 1&2
A GANGSTA'S PARADISE
By **Trai'Quan**

CAUGHT UP IN THE LIFE 1-3
THE STREETS NEVER LET GO 1-3
By **Robert Baptiste**

NEW TO THE GAME 1-3
MONEY, MURDER & MEMORIES 1-3
By **Malik D. Rice**

THE LIFE OF A HOOD STAR
By **Ca$h & Rashia Wilson**

THE STREETS WILL NEVER CLOSE 1-4
By **K'ajji**

LIFE OF A SAVAGE 1-4
A GANGSTA'S QUR'AN 1-4
MURDA SEASON 1-3
GANGLAND CARTEL 1-3
CHI'RAQ GANGSTAS 1-4
KILLERS ON ELM STREET 1-3
JACK BOYZ N DA BRONX 1-3
A DOPEBOY'S DREAM 1-3
JACK BOYS VS DOPE BOYS 1-3
COKE GIRLZ
COKE BOYS
SOSA GANG 1&2
BRONX SAVAGES
BODYMORE KINGPINS
BLOOD OF A GOON
By **Romell Tukes**

CREAM 2-3
THE STREETS WILL TALK
By **Yolanda Moore**

CONCRETE KILLA 1-3
VICIOUS LOYALTY 1-3
By **Kingpen**

THE ULTIMATE SACRIFICE 1-6
KHADIFI
IF YOU CROSS ME ONCE 1-5
ANGEL 1-4
IN THE BLINK OF AN EYE
By **Anthony Fields**

NIGHTMARES OF A HUSTLA 1-3
BLOOD AND GAMES 1&2
By **King Dream**

HARD AND RUTHLESS 1&2
MOB TOWN 251
THE BILLIONAIRE BENTLEYS 1-3
REAL G'S MOVE IN SILENCE
By **Von Diesel**

MOB TIES 1-7
SOUL OF A HUSTLER, HEART OF A KILLER 1-3
GORILLAZ IN THE TRENCHES
By **SayNoMore**

BODYMORE MURDERLAND 1-3
THE BIRTH OF A GANGSTER 1-4
By **Delmont Player**

FOR THE LOVE OF A BOSS 1&2
By **C. D. Blue**

KILLA KOUNTY 1-5
By **Khufu**

MOBBED UP 1-4
THE BRICK MAN 1-5
THE COCAINE PRINCESS 1-10
STEPPERS 1-3
SUPER GREMLIN 1-4
By **King Rio**

MONEY GAME 1&2
By **Smoove Dolla**

A GANGSTA'S KARMA 1-4
By **FLAME**

KING OF THE TRENCHES 1-3
By **GHOST & TRANAY ADAMS**

QUEEN OF THE ZOO 1&2
By **Black Migo**

GRIMEY WAYS 1-3
BETRAYAL OF A G
By **Ray Vinci**

XMAS WITH AN ATL SHOOTER
By **Ca$h & Destiny Skai**

KING KILLA 1&2
By **Vincent "Vitto" Holloway**

BETRAYAL OF A THUG 1&2
By **Fre$h**

A THUGGISH PASSION 2 | IRA B

THE MURDER QUEENS 1-6
By **Michael Gallon**

FOR THE LOVE OF BLOOD 1-4
By **Jamel Mitchell**

HOOD CONSIGLIERE 1&2
NO TIME FOR ERROR
By **Keese**

PROTÉGÉ OF A LEGEND 1&2
LOVE IN THE TRENCHES 1&2
By **Corey Robinson**

THE PLUG'S RUTHLESS DAUGHTER 1&2
By **Tony Daniels**

BORN IN THE GRAVE 1-3
CRIME PAYS 1&2
By **Self Made Tay**

MOAN IN MY MOUTH
By **XTASY**

TORN BETWEEN A GANGSTER AND A
GENTLEMAN
By **J-BLUNT & Miss Kim**

HERE TODAY GONE TOMORROW 1&2
By **Fly Rock**

PILLOW PRINCESS
By **S. Hawkins**

SANCTIFIED AND HORNY
by **XTASY**

WOMEN LIE MEN LIE 1-4
FIFTY SHADES OF SNOW 1-3
STACK BEFORE YOU SPLURGE
GIRLS FALL LIKE DOMINOES
NAÏVE TO THE STREETS
By **ROY MILLIGAN**

LOYALTY IS EVERYTHING 1-3
CITY OF SMOKE 1&2
By **Molotti**

THE BUTTERFLY MAFIA 1-4
SALUTE MY SAVAGERY 1&2
By **Fumiya Payne**

THE LANE 1&2
By **Ken-Ken Spence**

THE PUSSY TRAP 1-5
By **Nene Capri**

DIRTY DNA
By **Blaque**

BOOKS BY LDP'S CEO, CA$H

TRUST IN NO MAN
TRUST IN NO MAN 2
TRUST IN NO MAN 3
BONDED BY BLOOD
SHORTY GOT A THUG
THUGS CRY
THUGS CRY 2
THUGS CRY 3
TRUST NO BITCH
TRUST NO BITCH 2
TRUST NO BITCH 3
TIL MY CASKET DROPS
RESTRAINING ORDER
RESTRAINING ORDER 2
IN LOVE WITH A CONVICT
LIFE OF A HOOD STAR
XMAS WITH AN ATL SHOOTER